This book must be returned by the date specified at the time of issue as
the DATE DUE FOR RETURN.
The loan may be extended (personally, by post, telephone or online) for
a further period if the book is not required by another reader, by quoting
the above number / author / title.

Enquiries: 01709 336774

www.rotherham.gov.uk/libraries

SPECIAL MESSAGE TO READERS

THE ULVERSCROFT FOUNDATION
(registered UK charity number 264873)

was established in 1972 to provide funds for research, diagnosis and treatment of eye diseases. Examples of major projects funded by the Ulverscroft Foundation are:-

- The Children's Eye Unit at Moorfields Eye Hospital, London
- The Ulverscroft Children's Eye Unit at Great Ormond Street Hospital for Sick Children
- Funding research into eye diseases and treatment at the Department of Ophthalmology, University of Leicester
- The Ulverscroft Vision Research Group, Institute of Child Health
- Twin operating theatres at the Western Ophthalmic Hospital, London
- The Chair of Ophthalmology at the Royal Australian College of Ophthalmologists

You can help further the work of the Foundation by making a donation or leaving a legacy. Every contribution is gratefully received. If you would like to help support the Foundation or require further information, please contact:

THE ULVERSCROFT FOUNDATION
The Green, Bradgate Road, Anstey
Leicester LE7 7FU, England
Tel: (0116) 236 4325
website: www.foundation.ulverscroft.com

PIT AND THE PENDULUM

Peter 'Pit Bull' Geller is a ruined man
. . . A *wunderkind* at a Wall Street
investment bank, his constantly racing
mind started his downfall — a nervous
breakdown, caused by working twenty-
hour days, seven days a week. Then,
just as he was beginning to pull
himself together mentally, a taxi ran a
red light and hit him, crippling him
permanently. But despite his depen-
dence on alcohol and painkillers,
Peter's exceptional intelligence remains
intact — as many criminals find to
their cost . . . !

JOHN GREGORY BETANCOURT

PIT AND THE PENDULUM

Complete and Unabridged

LINFORD
Leicester

First published in Great Britain

First Linford Edition
published 2013

A catalogue record for this book is available
from the British Library.

ISBN 978–1–4448–1724–9

Published by
F. A. Thorpe (Publishing)
Anstey, Leicestershire

Set by Words & Graphics Ltd.
Anstey, Leicestershire
Printed and bound in Great Britain by
T.J. International Ltd., Padstow, Cornwall

This book is printed on acid-free paper

For Linda Landrigan, who is responsible for giving Pit his start.
And for my wife, Kim,
who is responsible for pretty much everything else.

1

Pit and the Pendulum

When the phone rang, I rolled over with a groan and reached for it. Who could possibly be calling me? I didn't have any friends left, and all my bills were paid up, thanks to last month's trip to Atlantic City's casinos.

''Lo?' I mumbled into the receiver. My head pounded something awful.

'Pit?' asked a man's voice.

I blinked. Nobody had called me that in years. 'Who is this?'

'Pit! Thank God I reached you — I need your help.'

'Huh.' I managed to sit up in bed. The room swayed; I felt sick and dizzy. 'What? Help? Who *is* this?'

'God, Pit, it's three o'clock! Aren't you awake?'

'What? Three o'clock?' With my free hand, I rubbed at crusty-feeling eyes. It didn't help. I felt old and tired and all fogged up inside . . . thirty years old and ready to die. 'Call me in the daytime!'

The voice on the phone chuckled. It sounded forced.

'Come on, Pit,' the man said urgently. 'It's three o'clock *in the afternoon*. Wake up. You're the sharpest guy I know. I need your help!'

Slowly I tried to think it through. Only frat brothers had ever called me Pit. Short for Pit-Bull — because I never let go. So that meant we had gone to college together, a lifetime or so ago. At most in any given year, our fraternity had thirty-two members. Times four . . . a lively selection of suspects.

'Pit? You still there?'

I frowned. A decade had deepened his voice, but it sounded familiar. Like a gear clicking into place, my brain started working and the name came to me: David Hunt. Tall, blond, and good-looking in a Calvin Klein-model sort of way, mostly skilled in partying and racket ball, but good enough academically to get his MBA without any special assistance from me. That was the only reason they let me into old Alpha Kappa, after all, to help the jocks and old-money frat boys keep up their GPAs. Sometimes I had resented it, being there to be used, but mostly I didn't care, since the perks were great. I got into all the parties. I had my share of dates and fun and beer, and I still graduated at the top of our class. So what if I did a lot of tutoring and ghost-writing?

David had been . . . fifty-third? Yes, that was right. Fifty-third in our graduating class. More than respectable for a party-boy from Alpha Kappa.

'What is it, Davy?' I said. The haze was lifting now. 'And I go by Peter these days.'

'Peter. Right. Come see me — I need your help. I'll make it worth your while.'

I yawned again. 'Where are you?'

'The Mackin Chase Hotel. I'll be in the lobby. Twenty minutes okay?'

'Make it an hour.'

'If I have to. But hurry.' A frantic note crept into his voice. 'My future depends on it.' He hung up.

Since he sounded desperate, I debated

skipping a shower. But one look in the mirror and a sniff at my armpits changed my mind: I could live with bloodshot eyes and mussed-up hair, but popular society frowned on people who smelled like I did right now.

Heaving my legs over the side of the bed, I found a bottle of aspirin on the night table and dry-swallowed four tablets. My right foot bumped against a half-empty bottle of Jack Daniels on the floor, and briefly I debated a wake-up shot. No, not now; I had an appointment to keep. Instead, I screwed the cap back on.

I spent the next fifteen minutes showering, shaving, and cleaning myself up for polite society. A gulp of half-flat Pepsi and a cold slice of pizza from the refrigerator made a very late breakfast. Then I found a shirt that wasn't too rumpled and put it on with jeans and comfortable old loafers. Finished, I grabbed a cane from the umbrella stand by the door, left my little one-bedroom Northwood apartment, and limped out to the Frankford El station.

A train came almost immediately,

luckily. It was mostly empty, so I flopped down in the corner — not the handicapped seat by the door, which I hate — and from there I proceeded to study the gum, scuff marks, and unidentifiable stains on the floor, trying not to look out the window at passing brick factories and endless lines of row-houses. Details tended to overwhelm me these days; that was partly what led to my nervous breakdown and retirement from a twenty-hours-a-day job at a Wall Street investment firm four years before. Now I kept to myself, tried not to leave my apartment when I didn't have to, and drank to blunt the pain and keep the edge off my always-racing mind.

Already it was starting. Everything I knew about David Chatham Hunt came bubbling up through my subconscious, whether relevant or not. The two classes we'd both taken together (Comp 104 and Introduction to Analytical Writing). His family crest, which he'd once shown me (a griffin on a shield, surrounded by Masonic-looking symbols). I could even name all seventeen girls he'd dated (and the two he'd bedded) while living at the frat house.

What could David Hunt possibly want with *me*? He came from a rich old family; his life should have been golden. Mellow, easy-going, never-a-worry-in-the-world Davy Hunt's greatest decision these days should have been which swimsuit model to date or which of his many Saabs and Porsches to drive.

The train tracks went underground, and the car got noisy and claustrophobic and dark. A dozen people joined me in the car. Almost there, almost there. I tried not to look at anyone else. I didn't want to figure out life stories from their clothes, tattoos, body-piercings, and jewelry.

* * *

I knew the Mackin Chase Hotel quite well, of course; it's a Philadelphia landmark, a towering glass-and-steel building near the intersection of 20th and Vine, five minutes' walk from the train station. Elevators ran up the outside of the building, and the roof had a helicopter pad. Several times I had wondered what the view would be like from up there. Several times I'd wondered what it would be like to jump.

I was ten minutes early for our appointment, but I strolled into the hotel lobby anyway. There, a modernistic fountain made of bent pieces of copper-colored sheet metal splashed and burbled amidst carefully groomed ferns and bamboo. Pale yellow carp swam lazily through a series of interlocking shallow pools. Around me, orchestral music played an incongruously up-tempo version of the Beatles' 'Yesterday.' How appropriate.

Davy Hunt, dressed all in black from his handmade Italian leather shoes to his mock turtleneck sweater and stylish leisure jacket, folded up the newspaper he'd been pretending to read and rose from a marble bench by the fountain. He forced a sickly grin as I hobbled toward him. His blond hair had grown longer and he now wore it combed to one side, trying to hide a receding hairline. When I got close, I saw the fine web of wrinkles around his eyes. But if he looked his age,

I knew I must look thirty years older than mine. Huffing a bit, I leaned on my cane and tried to look strong and brave. Or at least mentally competent.

'Pit — Peter, I mean. How are you doing?'

He stuck out his hand; I shook it automatically. His grip was a little too hard, and I rapidly extricated myself.

'I'm fine,' I lied.

'You look . . . well.' He swallowed hard, clearly shocked and appalled. Of course he remembered the old Peter Geller, the brilliant geek from college, who knew everything and never missed any detail, no matter how small. But those days were long gone.

'I know how I look, Davy-boy,' I said with a rueful grin. 'And well it isn't.'

'God, Pit!' he blurted out. 'What happened?'

I shrugged. 'Nervous breakdown. Spent six months in the psych ward. Got out, got hit by a taxi that ran a red light. I'm an alcoholic now — as well as a crip,' I added with wry humor. 'How about you?'

He sank down on the bench and buried

his face in his hands. For some reason, he seemed to be hyperventilating. His breath came in short gasps.

'God. I'm sorry, Pit. Peter. If I'd known — '

'Really, Davy, I don't mind.' I sat beside him and stretched out my legs. They hurt less that way. 'Want to tell me about it? I'll help if I can. I didn't have anything else planned for today.' Or ever.

'I — I can't ask you — '

'Sure you can. Isn't that what frat brothers are for?' I didn't add: even second-class ones like me? 'So. Tell me what's wrong.'

His ice-blue eyes searched mine for a minute. He must really have been desperate, since he gave a nod. I smiled encouragingly.

'Blackmail,' he whispered. His shoulders hunched. 'I'm being blackmailed.'

'Oh?' I raised my eyebrows. 'Start at the beginning,' I said. So much for the squeaky-clean kid I'd known in college. What had he gotten himself into?

'Okay, Pit.' He looked around. 'But not here.'

'Where, then? Your home? Or your office? You *do* have an office?'

He glanced at the lobby bar — Mack's Place — which was open and doing a modest business with the pre-dinner crowd. But then he hesitated. Probably didn't want to throw fuel on the fire of my alcoholism, so to speak.

'Come on,' I said, levering myself upright with my cane. Best get things moving. 'You can buy me a ginger ale while you fill me in.'

'Are you doing that seven-step thing?' he asked carefully.

'It's twelve steps, and no.' I grinned back at him over my shoulder. 'I'm quite happy being a drunk. Alcohol kills the pain better than Tylenol and morphine. But I can take a day off for an old friend.'

'Um. Thanks.' Clearly that disconcerted him.

He grabbed his newspaper and trailed me into Mack's. Most of the customers sat at the bar, so I picked a booth at the rear. When a waitress appeared (Cindy, said her nametag: bleached blond hair, fake fingernails, maybe twenty, looked

10

like a college student from the University of Pennsylvania) I kept my word and ordered ginger ale, even though I felt the shakes coming on. Davy asked for scotch and soda. We sat in silence until Cindy served us.

'So?' I said again. I leaned back and sucked soda through a thin red straw. Nasty stuff. 'Fill me in. How can I help?'

Davy folded his hands and leaned forward. 'I told you I was being blackmailed.'

'Sex, drugs, or murder?' I asked lightly. It was hard keeping a straight face. I couldn't imagine the David Hunt I'd known involved in anything shady.

'Gambling. There's a private club out on the Main Line. I was there with a girl a few weeks back . . . ' He shrugged. 'Had a few too many drinks, and before I knew it, I was twenty thousand in the hole. I left a marker for it. Didn't want it showing up on my credit card statement — you understand.'

'Just pay it off. You have the cash, don't you?'

'Sure. But I can't pay it off. Someone beat me to it.'

Davy reached into the inside pocket of his jacket, pulled out a piece of paper, and slid it across the table. When I unfolded it, I found a color laser printout of a series of eight small pictures, four on each side. From the graininess, the shots must have been taken with one of those hide-in-your-palm micro cameras. Seven showed Davy gambling: craps, roulette, blackjack. In half of them, he had a drop-dead gorgeous blonde on his arm. The eighth was a picture of an I.O.U. to the Greens Club bearing his signature — $20,000.

'Who's the lady?' I scrutinized the blonde's face, but I had never seen her before.

'A friend of mine. Her name's Cree.'

'Actress-slash-model?' She had that under-nourished look. And breasts that defied gravity.

He shifted uneasily. 'Yes.'

'You aren't wearing a wedding ring. She's not your wife. So that can't be the problem.'

He stared at me. 'You don't read the *Inquirer*, do you?'

'Not often.' Not in the last four years, anyway.

'Here.' He picked up his newspaper, opened it to the second page of the business section, folded it back, and slid it across to me.

DRESHER NATIVE DAVID C. HUNT, JR. CONFIRMED FOR HUNT INDUSTRIES BOARD OF DIRECTORS

So read a small headline. I skimmed the brief article. My friend Davy just joined the family business, it seemed.

Nodding, I looked up. 'Congrats. But what does this have to do with blackmail?'

'Last year, there were . . . scandals in the company.' He shook his head. 'I can't believe you missed it. The chief financial officer is in jail. The chief operating officer plea-bargained his way to fines and probation. Half the accountants are under federal indictment. Dad barely fought off being forced out as CEO. He had to struggle to get me nominated to the Board of Directors last week. The merest hint of a scandal and they'll yank me out. So . . . these pictures and my marker have to stay buried.'

13

'You should go to the police.' I added pointedly, 'Blackmail *is* illegal.'

He lowered his voice. 'So is gambling in unlicensed clubs. If investors think I'm financially irresponsible, I'll be yanked off the board — and, well, that will crush Dad. There's been a Hunt at the top of the company for a hundred and ten years. He's counting on me to take over when I have more experience. This is the first step.'

'Point taken.' You couldn't argue with parental expectations. 'So what do you want *me* to do?'

'I need someone to handle the payoff for me. Someone I can trust who doesn't have his own agenda. My friends — well, let's say they're friends of convenience. If they scent blood in the water . . . they're as likely to turn me in to the tabloids as the blackmailer is.'

I nodded; that I could understand. 'But why *me*?'

'I saw your name in that alumni rag a few weeks ago — it said you were back in Philadelphia.' He shrugged. 'You were the most straight-as-an-arrow guy I ever met.

That whole 'moral compass' thing they teach in business ethics — that's you to a tee. I thought . . . ' He choked up.

'That was a long time ago, Davy-boy.'

'I know, Pit. I . . . I'm sorry to have bothered you.' He stood, snatching up the laser printout and the newspaper.

I grabbed his arm. 'Come back here. Geez, you're touchy. Of course I'll help.'

He hesitated a moment, then sat heavily. If he hadn't been so desperate, I knew he would have run.

'Pit . . . ' He leaned forward, voice dropping. 'Look at yourself. You're a mess. Your hands are shaking. You can barely walk. This isn't a game. I appreciate your offer, but — '

'I know I have problems,' I said, 'but I can still help you. That's what friends are for.' I looked at him, my eyes pleading. I needed this. Needed something to do, something special to distract me from the downswing toward unhappy oblivion that was my life.

He took a deep breath, then sagged a little and seemed to give in. 'Okay. But — '

I cut him off. 'Start at the beginning and tell me everything. I assume there's a letter with payment instructions. If so, I want to see it.'

'Here.' He pulled another piece of paper from his jacket pocket and slid it across the table. I unfolded it carefully. It had been written on a computer, typed in twelve-point Arial, and printed on the type of generic white copier paper you could get at any Staples or OfficeMax.

david
you can redeem your marker for two hundred thousand dollars if you agree place an ad in the *inquirer* that reads single white elephant named dumbo seeking mate you will get a voice mail with delivery instructions
a friend

I retrieved the printout of the pictures, spread it flat on the table, and studied each image one at a time, committing faces to memory.

'What about this Cree woman?' I asked.

'I've dated her off and on for two years.

She's a bit shallow, but okay. Focused on her career. Expects to marry me in a year or two. At least, we've been talking about it.'

'So you don't think she's behind it?'

'For a mere two hundred thou? Come on, I'm worth fifty million all by myself. If she waits, she'll have it all.'

'Not with a prenuptial agreement.'

He chuckled. 'The jewelry I bought her last month is worth more than that!'

'All right. It's not her. Was there anything else? A threat to send everything to the newspapers? Or your company's Board of Directors?'

'Nothing *specific*. But I know that's what they'll do if I don't pay up.'

I chewed my lip. 'Did you save the envelope the letter came in, by any chance?'

'No. Why? Is it important?'

'I want to know where it was mailed from.'

'Sorry, no return address.'

'Postmark?'

'Philadelphia.'

'Zip code?'

17

'I didn't notice.'

Not much help; it's a big city.

I asked, 'When does the ad run?'

He tapped the newspaper on the table. 'It's in today's classifieds. I just looked it up.'

'Any voice mails yet?'

He nodded. 'A few ladies looking for dates so far. The Dumbo part seems to have tickled their fancy.'

I rotated the page with the pictures and pointed to the one where Davy stood by the roulette table. A man in the background had caught my eye: a little older than us, salt-and-pepper hair, small mustache . . . the sort you'd never look at twice.

'Do you recognize him?' I asked.

Davy leaned forward, squinted. 'No. Why?'

'He's looking straight at whoever took the picture. And look — he's standing behind you and Cree at the blackjack table, too. And in this shot — you can't see his face, but that's clearly his suit. He was stalking you.'

'Say, I think you're right! But it still

doesn't help. I don't know him.'

I nodded. 'All right.' My mind was already turning through the possibilities. Too bad I didn't know anyone at the police department or the FBI. Face-recognition software was the latest thing. A name would be helpful. Who else might know him? The gambling club's management?

Davy leaned forward and touched my hand. 'Listen to me, Pit,' he said seriously. 'I didn't ask you here to solve a crime. This isn't a puzzle to work out. Your job is to be a courier. That's it. Once the payoff is made, you have to drop it.'

I smiled. 'I understand, Davy. I'm just naturally curious.'

'I don't want you doing anything stupid and getting hurt. Don't be a pit-bull. Just help me out — I'll make it worth your while.'

He slid a cell phone across to me, along with a set of car keys. 'Just hit redial. The password on the account is 9-1-1-9.'

'What are the keys for?'

'My car. It's valet parked — the claim check is on the key ring, see? That plastic chit on the end. Uh, you *can* still drive, can't you?'

'Sure, I just have to be careful.'

'Good.'

'And the money?'

'In the trunk,' he said, 'in a briefcase.'

I stared at him in disbelief. 'Are you crazy? What if the parking attendant rips you off?'

He grinned. 'I gave him a valet key — it only opens the driver's door and starts the ignition. No way for him to open the trunk.'

I nodded and said: 'So I take them the money, get back your marker, and see that all the files for the digital pictures are destroyed. Is that the plan?'

'Uh-huh.'

'One last question.'

'Shoot.'

'Where is this gambling club?'

'Why?'

'Just curious. I like to gamble, and it's closer than Atlantic City. It's not like they can blackmail *me*!'

Grudgingly, he told me. Then he glanced at his watch and frowned.

'Some place you have to be?' I asked.

'Yeah. Dad's giving a dinner in my honor tonight. The whole Board will be there. I have to get going or I'm going to be late. Cree is picking me up in about two minutes. Can you handle things?'

'Sure.' I gave a quick grin. 'You can count on me, Davy. I'll take care of everything.'

'I know.' He smiled — a bit wistfully, I thought. 'You haven't even asked what's in it for you. You'd make a bad business-man, Pit.'

I laughed. 'Must be our old Alpha Kappa bond. You don't owe me a thing, Davy-boy. I'll help because I can.'

'Thanks. I mean it, Pit. *Thanks*.'

* * *

He left, stopping briefly at the bar to pay our tab. I waited till he was gone, then eased myself out of the booth with the help of my cane, scooped up keys and cell phone, and headed for the lobby.

Already a plan was forming in the back of my mind. There was a small barber

21

shop off the hotel lobby, next to the gift store: forty bucks for a simple haircut, but I needed to look my best tonight. I was going to pay the gambling club a visit.

The barber did an adequate job of neatening me up. Then I went to the men's room and used wet paper towels to clean all the hairs off my face, neck, and ears that he missed.

After that, I went to the gift shop and poked around until I found a travel kit that included a small pair of scissors. I paid for it, pocketed the scissors, then threw out the nail clippers and everything else. I paused long enough by a trash can to cut mustache-man's picture out of the printout. Maybe I'd get lucky and find out his name when I asked around at the gambling club tonight. That's where I intended to go . . . straight to the heart of the problem.

Then I exited the hotel. Instead of retrieving Davy's car from the parking attendant, I headed for the men's clothing shop I'd passed a block or so down. Time for a suit . . . something expensive and Italian, maybe silk. And a flashy tie. I wanted to look like I had a million bucks tonight.

It seemed to me Davy's situation had two possible causes. One, blackmailers had recognized him, picked him as an easy mark, and surreptitiously photographed him at the gambling club. Two, the management of the gambling club had set him up and was conducting this sting. To get him deep enough in debt to leave an I.O.U., they would probably have to be running crooked games. And I counted on my own skills with numbers and general mental abilities to be able to spot bad dice, rigged tables, or marked cards. Either way, the casino seemed the logical place to start.

As I walked, I used Davy's cell phone to check for voice-mail messages. Nothing new.

* * *

Two hours later, and $3,700 dollars poorer thanks to my credit cards and rush tailoring, I had an Armani suit that fit like a glove. Thank God for credit cards. I had traded in my cane for a silver-handled walking stick. And a small blood-red carnation brightened my lapel. As I glanced at my reflection in the side windows of shops, I had to admit I didn't look like the same seedy cripple who had agreed to do this job.

I had a car to get . . . my first driving experience since the accident . . . and I had blackmailers to catch. Whether Davy wanted it or not, I intended to help him the best way I could. And that meant making sure his enemies couldn't hold anything over him for the rest of his life. If he paid off this time, I knew they would be back in a few months for more . . . and more . . . and more.

★   ★   ★

Davy's car wasn't the bright red Ferrari I'd half expected, but a black BMW sports car, low-slung and sexy. It had a manual transmission, but after a few jerky starts the rhythm of driving one came back to me, and I pulled out onto Vine and accelerated smoothly toward the

Main Line and the old-money towns west of Philadelphia.

What should have been a twenty-minute ride took nearly four times as long, thanks to an overwhelming volume of rush hour traffic on Route 76. When I finally pulled off at the proper exit, it was growing dark. I began scanning street signs. Half a dozen turns later, I found myself on a private road heading for what was marked as a members-only golf course. And sure enough it had acres of floodlit greens to the sides and back, along with a sprawling clubhouse, a catering hall and half a dozen other barn-like outbuildings, and ample parking lots lit by bright floodlights.

It was still early for the fashionable set, but even so, the last building — which Davy claimed was the casino — seemed to be doing a lively business. Quite a few vehicles were parked outside its entrance, and a pair of teenage boys manned a valet station at the curb.

I parked myself, retrieved the black leather briefcase from the trunk, flipped its latches, and peeked inside at bundles of crisp hundred dollar bills. Two thousand of them, if my math was right. And it was.

Turning, I limped across the lot toward the casino. At the door, a security camera panned down slightly to take me in. There was no doorman waiting, so I tried the knob. Locked, of course. I pressed a small brass buzzer. Moments later, a window set in the door slid open.

'Yeah?' said a man with brown eyes and weather-bronzed skin. 'What is it?' He had a heavy New Jersey accent.

'Swordfish?' I volunteered.

'Don't play with me.'

He must not have seen many Marx Brothers movies. Or perhaps he'd heard the line so many times he no longer found it humorous.

'Sorry,' I said. 'I'd like in, please.'

'This is a private club.'

'I was invited by a member. Perhaps you know him.' I juggled my cane a second, then flipped the latches on the briefcase and held it up so he and the camera could see. 'His name is cash.'

The eyes widened slightly in surprise.

'Who's the real friend, wise guy?' Jersey-boy demanded.

'Well, if you must know, David Hunt.'

'He's not a member.'

I shrugged. 'He was here a few days ago and spoke glowingly of the action.'

'He's not a member.'

'Then refer me to the sales department.'

'Membership is by invitation only.' He seemed determined to make things difficult.

I said, 'Bump me up a step on the food chain, and I'll get myself invited.' I gave him a smile. 'Besides, won't you get in trouble if you let me walk away with all this money? I'm sure others are watching on your security cameras.'

The window slammed shut. For a moment, I wondered if I'd pissed him off. Finally, though, I heard a deadbolt slide over and the door swung out. My personal charms must have worked.

Jersey-boy was about forty, of Mediterranean descent, and built like a brick wall. He wore his hair short and slicked back, and a thin white scar ran from his left ear to his chin. From the bulge under his suit jacket, I knew he sported a shoulder holster. I got the impression he could have torn me in half without really trying. This definitely wasn't the sort of person I wanted to tangle with.

'In,' he said with a jerk of his thumb.

'Thanks.'

I shut the briefcase and strolled into a richly decorated antechamber perhaps ten feet deep and twenty feet wide. From plush red carpet to oak paneled walls to the crystal chandelier overhead, everything felt rich and inviting. Even the paintings on the walls were tasteful country landscapes. The air had the well-scrubbed feel of industrial air conditioning.

'Sit,' he said, indicating a low bench, its seat done in crushed red velvet the same shade as the carpet.

I sat, briefcase beside me, cane across my knees. It hurt, but I kept my legs folded back. A small table held recent issues of *Newsweek*, *Cosmopolitan*, and *Sports Illustrated*. None looked like it had ever been read. I picked through them. The subscription address labels had been meticulously clipped out.

After a couple of minutes, four people trooped through after me: two middle-aged men in tuxedos, two women in evening gowns. Jersey-boy greeted them warmly. I felt underdressed until I recalled the photos Davy had shown me. Most men in the club had been wearing suits. Gambling wasn't necessarily a black-tie event here.

The newcomers passed through a doorway to my left, into a short windowless hallway. Jersey-boy resumed his post by the entrance.

Then the door on the other end of the room opened, and an older man in a gray silk suit appeared. White hair, brushed straight back, dark Mediterranean complexion, trim and wiry looking — and I knew him. Somehow, somewhere, we had met before. *But where?* I began to search my memories.

He gave a slight nod to the muscle on duty.

'Mr. Smith will see you now,' Jersey-boy told me.

'Thanks.' I used my cane and limped toward Smith. He turned to lead the way up another red-carpeted hall.

As I passed through the doorway, I caught a whiff of Smith's lavender cologne. Then beefy men on either side grabbed my arms in vice-like grips. I gave a startled yelp and dropped both cane and briefcase. They half carried, half dragged me forward.

I should have seen the trap. Davy's money made a very tempting target.

When I glanced back, a fourth man was picking up my briefcase and cane. He trailed us.

The two goons brought me to a small room with a chest-high wooden table pushed up against the back wall. Hand-held metal detectors and other equipment sat there. Of course — they had to check me out to make sure I wasn't an FBI agent of some sort. I let myself relax a bit. Maybe this wouldn't take long and we could get down to business.

The fourth man set my cane and briefcase down next to the table, then frisked me. He removed Davy's cell phone and my billfold, then turned to the table and selected one of the metal detectors. Switching it on with his thumb, he stepped forward and ran it over my body with practiced efficiency, starting at my head and working his way down. Each time the device beeped, one of the goons removed the offending bit of metal and tossed it onto the table: car keys, house keys, cufflinks. They even took my belt for its buckle.

As his men worked, Smith picked up my billfold and went through it item by item. Where *had* I seen him before? Strangely, the fact that I couldn't identify him bothered me more than the search. I could usually place any name or face in a few seconds.

Several times Smith murmured, 'Hmm.' Once was when he held my driver's license — probably in reaction to my address. No one with money lived where I lived. He pulled a small notepad from his back pocket and jotted something down.

Then the metal detector hit my legs and went wild. Everyone jumped. The goons' grip on my arms became painful.

'I have pins in my bones,' I gasped. 'That's why I need a cane.'

'Kick off your shoes and drop your pants,' the man with the metal detector said in a not-to-be-argued-with voice.

I did so. I could feel the tension go out of the room as their gazes dropped from my gray briefs to the hideously scarred, vaguely fleshy mess of my legs. I looked like something out of a freak show. Pity — oh how well I knew pity. And revulsion. I saw it now in their faces. It had taken six operations to make my lower limbs at all usable after the accident. For a while, every doctor I saw told me I'd need the right one amputated. Stubbornly, I had refused. They had also told me I'd never walk again.

'There are,' I continued to break the sudden and uncomfortable silence, 'seventeen steel pins in my right leg and eight in my left. I can point them all out, if it's helpful.'

'Not necessary.' The man with the metal detector ran it over my shoes. Apparently the nails were too small to register, or he had adjusted his equipment for them. Then he took my pants and searched them before giving them back.

'He's clean,' he told Smith.

'Check the bag and the cane,' said Smith. He nodded to the goons, who released me. I had to lean against the wall to get my pants up. It hurt enough to make my eyes swim, but I kept my face calm and impassive.

'Mr. Geller,' said Smith. He tossed my billfold to me. 'You have a most unusual way of making an entrance.'

'I realize that, sir.'

'You understand, we have to be careful about who we let in.'

'Of course.' I shuffled to the table, leaned on it heavily, and recovered my keys, cufflinks, and belt. Slowly I put everything back.

'His cane is fine,' said the man examining it. 'So is his bag. Lots of money in it.'

'How much?' Smith asked.

'Want me to count it, sir?'

'Don't bother,' I said. 'It's two hundred thousand even.'

Smith raised his eyebrows. 'That's

quite a lot to carry around. Not that I'm complaining, of course. Games always work in the house's favor.'

'I didn't come to gamble,' I said. 'I came to meet with the person in charge. I assume that's you.'

He inclined his head slightly, eyes narrowing. 'Yes.'

'So — ' I smiled. Hopefully he would go for it. 'How about a meeting?'

He studied me for a moment, undoubtedly trying to figure out my angle. Apparently he didn't find me the least bit intimidating. I just wished I could remember where we had met.

Then, suddenly, it came back to me. At the Golden Nugget Casino in Atlantic City, right after they released me from rehab.

I had braces on both legs and had to be helped onto my stool at the blackjack table by casino attendants. I was on painkillers, heavy ones, and I seemed to be viewing the world through a haze.

Smith had watched me play for half an hour, winning steadily. I had about forty thousand in chips in front of me when he approached, leaned forward, and whispered in my ear, 'The house doesn't mind regulars who win small amounts. It's card-counters who try to take them for a fortune that gets the house upset.'

I had glanced at his nametag — 'C. Tortelli' — as I nodded. 'Thanks,' I said. Even through my painkiller haze, I understood.

Maybe it had been charity for a cripple. Maybe he had just been a good guy. But I took his suggestion.

The hospitals and doctors had sucked my insurance, then my savings dry at that point, and I needed money. A lot of it. And I needed a consistent source for more, too. If the casinos blacklisted me, I realized, I would never get back inside them.

I spent the next ten minutes losing steadily, like I'd had a run of luck that went sour. I left with twenty thousand instead of forty or fifty. And ever since, I kept my winnings to two thousand dollars, more or less, per casino per monthly visit. And so I managed to keep myself both afloat and under their radar.

All thanks to Mr. Smith here. Or 'C. Tortelli,' as his nametag once said.

Now Smith/Tortelli said, 'Very well. I'm intrigued, Mr. Geller. This way, please.'

★　★　★

Two minutes later we sat in an office that might have belonged to any mid-level executive at any big corporation: heavy walnut desk, computer, pictures of wife and kids in silver frames, signed baseball on a little wooden stand. He even had an inbox and an outbox. Who knew organized crime had such amenities.

'Drink?' he asked.

'Water, please.'

He handed me a bottle of Poland Spring water from a tiny refrigerator in the corner, next to a small wet bar. I peeled the plastic wrapper off the spout and took a sip, spilling a little. My hands were shaking again.

'So,' he prompted, settling down behind his desk, 'you say you're not here to gamble.'

'That's right.' Without preamble, I told

him Davy Hunt's blackmail story. 'It occurred to me,' I said in conclusion, 'that there are only three possibilities. One is that your little operation here is behind the blackmail scheme, and that you're using the casino to set up unsuspecting men like David Hunt. In which case, I'll just cut out the middleman and leave you the money now. Payment in full. Destroy the pictures and we're done.'

He leaned back in his chair, steepling his fingers. 'What's the second possibility?' he asked.

'That rogue members of your staff are doing it on the sly. In which case, you need to be informed so you can act to stop it. Or, if you prefer, cut yourself in on the action. Once you remove David Hunt, of course, from the target list.'

He nodded slowly. 'And the third?'

'That you and your staff are unwitting victims. After all, your club's reputation will be severely damaged if word gets out that members are being photographed and blackmailed. This is my personal suspicion, of course.'

'Of course.' He looked off into the

distance thoughtfully. 'I don't suppose you know who's behind this blackmail plot.'

'Possibly.' I reached into my jacket pocket and fished out the clipped picture of mustache-man. 'There are at least two people working the setup. One arranges the shots, the other snaps photos with one of those micro spy cameras.'

Smith took the picture. From the way his eyes widened slightly, I knew he recognized mustache-man. And he was trying hard not to show it.

'I've seen him,' he said slowly. 'He comes in once or twice a week, and he drops a couple hundred each time. Not a big spender, but the sort of solid repeat customer we like.'

He put the clipped picture into his vest pocket instead of returning it. Then he rose.

'Thank you for coming to me,' he said. 'I'll handle things. You can tell Mr. Hunt that he won't be bothered again.'

I nodded and rose. He did not offer to shake hands, nor did he offer to return Davy's money. *Quid pro quo*; he could keep it with my blessing if it got Davy safely off the hook. Davy didn't need the cash as much as he needed security.

'Do you gamble, Mr. Geller?' he asked unexpectedly.

'Now and again, Mr. Tortelli.'

He didn't react to my using his real name. Instead, he handed me a small piece of paper.

'What's this?' I asked. It had '10K — S' written on it.

Instead of answering, he pressed a hidden button under his desktop. A second later, the door opened. Goon number two stood there.

'Sir?'

'Mr. Geller has a chit for ten thousand dollars. Make sure he has a good time. He's going to be my guest tonight.' Then he turned back to me. 'I suggest you play at table number five. Find a comfortable seat and relax.'

★ ★ ★

Smith's personal invitation opened all the right doors. The goon smiled a perfect shark's smile as he escorted me through several hallways to a cavernous casino done all in reds and golds. Roulette, baccarat, blackjack, poker, craps, and other table games occupied the center of the room. Jangling slot machines lined the walls. Cashier's stations at both ends of the room doled out a steady supply of chips, while scantily clad women circulated with trays of drinks. Keep the alcohol flowing and the money will follow: it seemed like a sound business plan. A hundred or so people were already inside, moving from game to game.

'This is table 5,' said the goon, halting at a low-rent blackjack table. The dealer, a middle-aged woman, was shuffling eight fresh decks in preparation for filling a card shoe. Three of the five seats were already taken.

'Thanks.' When I settled onto one of the empty stools, I found I had a nice view of the whole room. I put Tortelli's chit in front of me, and without batting an eye the dealer slid over several tall stacks of red, blue, and black chips. They had values stamped in gold from $5 to

$100. I didn't bother to count them.

For the next few hours, I played slowly and conservatively, adding more chips than I lost to my stacks. I kept my eyes open and my mouth shut. This was business, I told myself. Tortelli wouldn't have put me here without cause. With half my attention on the game, I surveyed the crowds and began picking out plain-clothes security. I found six of them. And a couple I suspected, but couldn't quite confirm.

Then I saw him — mustache-man! He strutted in with a middle-aged woman on his arm. Both of them dressed conservatively, with bland haircuts and dull watches, rings, and jewelry. No one would have looked at them twice.

The dealer placed a king and a five in front of me.

'Hit,' I said, tapping the table.

She dealt me an eight — busted. While she finished out the other players' hands, I leaned back and watched as a subtle change came over the movements of the crowd. Three people converged on my blackmail suspects.

A passing woman deliberately spilled her drink on mustache-man and — though I couldn't hear her voice over the noise of the room — began to apologize profusely, brushing him off with a cocktail napkin. A couple of security guards appeared and, with sympathy, escorted the pair off, I assumed under the pretense of getting the man dried off. Perhaps even promises of free chips to help ease the distress . . . anything to keep a regular happy.

I rose and tossed the blackjack dealer a $50 chip. 'Thanks,' I said. 'Cashing out now.'

'Thank *you!*' she replied, smiling for the first time since I'd sat down. She handed me a small dish, and I scooped my winnings into it.

Then I headed after mustache-man and his date. But Goon One and Goon Two cut me off before I reached the door. They simply blocked my way, folded their arms, and smiled their sharky smiles.

'Hello again, boys,' I said, smiling back. I could play the polite game, too.

'Mr. Smith says you should go back and gamble,' Two said, tapping the little brown earplug he now wore.

'And miss the fun?' I leaned forward and spoke into Two's lapel. He had to have a microphone in there somewhere. 'I have a vindictive streak, Mr. Tortelli. I like to see things properly finished. No loose ends.'

Goon Two said, 'Mr. Smith doesn't think you should be an accessory to what's happening. Play cards or go home. This isn't a game now.'

That's what I needed to hear. I nodded and spoke again to his lapel.

'Very well. I'm done, and thanks.'

Tortelli had it wrong. It *was* a game. Mustache-man was one player, and Davy was the other. All the rest of us . . . we were merely pawns on the board.

I handed Two my tray of chips. Turning, I limped toward the door. It was one thing to orchestrate Davy's victory, but quite another to actually execute it. Or see it executed.

I did not want to know the details.

★ ★ ★

I had thought to simply return to my old life after that, but — as they say — events conspired against me. The next morning Davy phoned, and I assured him that his problem had been taken care of.

'Thanks,' he said, sounding relieved. 'Then it went well?'

'Better than I had hoped. I don't think we'll be hearing from the blackmailers again.'

'How did you like the car?'

I laughed. 'Nice. Took me a few minutes to get back into driving stick, but don't worry, the transmission's fine.'

He chuckled. 'Good. Stop by my office. I have some paperwork for you.'

'What sort?' I couldn't imagine needing paperwork for eliminating a blackmail threat.

'Sometimes, Pit, you're pretty dense for a genius. I told you I'd take care of you. I'm giving you the car, with my thanks. Just a matter of signing the registration over.'

My heart skipped. That had to be a forty thousand dollar vehicle.

'I can't accept,' I said. 'It's too much,

and I'm a public transit sort of guy. Buy me lunch sometime instead, okay?'

'Pit . . . '

'I mean it,' I said firmly. 'I enjoyed helping, Davy. I don't get out enough. Give me your address, and I'll drop the car off this afternoon.'

★ ★ ★

That should have ended matters. I dropped off the car at the center city office building where Davy had his office, accepted his invitation for dinner that Sunday (Cree apparently liked to cook; she didn't eat, but she was a master of Cajun cuisine).

The train ride home was uneventful. I got my favorite corner seat after a couple of stops, and I even managed to look out the window as we headed for the Frankfort station. So much for being a cripple. I had accomplished my mission with flying colors.

I limped to my apartment five blocks from the El station, unlocked the dead-bolt, and paused in the doorway. Something was wrong. I always left a light on in the kitchen, and it was off. Instead, the bedroom light was on. Someone had been here. I paused, listening, and heard a slight creak from my sofa. Broken springs could be useful sometimes.

Then I caught a faint whiff of lavender.

'Reach out to your right,' I said, 'and turn on the lamp, Mr. Tortelli. I like to see my guests.'

There followed a half-second silence, then two sharp clicks as he turned the switch. A dim yellow bulb came on, revealing my Spartan living room: worn yellow sofa, two white-and-yellow wingback chairs, wooden coffee table, two tall bookcases mostly devoted to bric-a-brac. As the lamp's fluorescent bulb began to warm, the light steadily increased.

Tortelli leaned back, watching me. He wore another silk suit, dark blue this time with pin stripes. His tie glistened faintly, like sharkskin. Even his black shoes had an enviable shine.

'Two seconds in the dark to realize you had an intruder, identify him, and conclude you weren't in danger. Very good,

Mr. Geller. Very good indeed.'

'Not in danger? You understate your abilities, Mr. Tortelli.'

He half shrugged modestly. 'Perhaps.'

I came in and closed the door. Casually I glanced around the room, taking inventory . . . not that I owned anything worth stealing. Every object in the room had been moved slightly out of place; it would take hours to put them back. And the changes were so slight that few others would have noticed — or cared.

'Why the search?' I asked. 'What were you hoping to find?'

'You knew my name,' he said. 'My old name. I haven't used it in nearly three years. I need to know how.'

'We met in Atlantic City when you worked at the Golden Nugget.' I eased myself into a chair, wincing a bit. Then I told him my casino-enlightenment story. 'Of course,' I went on, 'your hair is a bit different, and your clothes are vastly better these days. You've really come up in the world.'

'And you remembered me, even after all these years?' He looked surprised. 'I must have made quite an impression on you.'

'No.' I leaned forward. 'I remember everything and everyone, Mr. Tortelli. It's a curse. Oh, sorry, I'm a bad host. If you'd like a drink, please help yourself. Beer in the fridge, hard stuff over the sink. I'm not up to waiting on anyone. Need to catch my breath.'

'Still . . . ' He rose and began to pace. 'It took quite a bit of effort to find out about you, Mr. Geller. Or may I call you Pit?'

'If you like. Charles? Or Charlie?'

'Cal.'

'Ah.' So much for 'C. Tortelli' on his nametag. 'See? I don't know everything.'

'I don't like loose ends, Pit. I imagine you don't, either.'

'Sometimes I do.' I tensed, but tried not to show it. Was I a loose end, to be rubbed out in my own apartment?

He seemed to sense my unease and chuckled. 'I like you, 'Pit-Bull' Peter Geller. You have a unique style.' He reached into his jacket pocket and pulled out a small, almost square bit of plastic, which he flipped onto the coffee table.

It was a flash memory card for a digital camera. I leaned forward with interest.

'From the blackmailers?'

'Yes. As far as I can tell, it contains the originals of their pictures. There don't appear to be any copies.'

'Thank you,' I said.

He nodded once, then rose and started for the door. Halfway out, he paused. 'You turned down Hunt's offer of a car. May I ask why?'

How did he know that? My phone had to be bugged. I'd deal with it later.

I said, 'I don't need a car. The insurance premiums would eat me alive. And this isn't the right neighborhood for a BMW, anyway. Wouldn't last a week on the street.'

He nodded. 'Interesting. Thank you, Pit. I'll be in touch.'

A shiver ran through me at those words. But then he closed the door and was gone. And somehow, I didn't feel like drinking.

2

Pit on the road to hell

When the telephone rang, I rolled over and squinted blearily in its general direction, my head swimming from too much whisky the night before. What was this, Grand Central Station? I'd gotten more phone calls in the last week than I had in the entire previous year.

Cursing would-be friends and telemarketers under my breath, I fumbled for the handset. Though booze helped blunt the pain from my ruined legs, the side effects left a lot to be desired. My coordination was off, and I couldn't stop my hands from shaking.

Somehow, I got the receiver up to my ear. 'Who is this?' I rasped.

'Hello, Pit,' said a too-smooth voice.

I felt the blood drain from my face. Gulping hard, I sat up, nearly dropping the phone.

That voice belonged to Cal Tortelli — or Mr. Smith, as he now called himself. He ran an illegal gambling club outside Philadelphia. When an old college friend of mine fell victim to a blackmail scheme, I had manipulated Smith into handling the problem for us. I didn't know all the details, but I knew the resolution had been neither legal nor pretty for the blackmailers.

Unfortunately, Smith seemed to have taken a particular interest in me. He had researched my life, even going so far as to have my phone bugged. I seemed to intrigue him . . . probably due to my trick memory. I could recall every name, date, face, and fact that I had ever encountered.

'Hello, Mr. Smith,' I said warily. 'What do you want?'

'Don't you ever leave your apartment?' he asked with a low chuckle.

'I try not to. Walking hurts.'

'Come outside. I need to see you.'

'You're . . . *here*?'

'Yes.' He paused. 'And bring your toothbrush, 'Pit-bull' Peter Geller. You're

51

going on a trip.' He hung up.

With an uneasy feeling, I fumbled my phone back into its cradle. I really needed to get an answering machine and start screening calls. Mr. Smith was the last person I wanted to meet again . . . in my book, he ranked somewhere south of doctors and lawyers.

Bring a toothbrush? Why a toothbrush, but not a change of clothes?

No sense guessing. Throwing off my blanket, I hauled the hideously scarred pieces of flesh that now passed for my legs over the edge of the bed and, with a groan and several grunts, levered myself to a standing position. From the arches of my feet to the joints of my hips, I ached with a dull constant pain. Getting up was the worst part of any day.

I eyed the nearly-empty bottle of Jack Daniels on the pillow next to mine. Maybe one quick drink, just to steady my nerves? No, I had better not . . . Tortelli/ Smith was a sharp man, and I'd need my head clear to deal with him.

Taking a deep breath, I glanced around my Spartan bedroom: bed, dresser, night stand, closet with shut doors. No pictures, no calendars, no clock — time doesn't mean much when you're waiting to die. Nothing had been moved; nobody had been inside while I slept.

I felt my attention starting to sharpen, all the little details leaping out at me. It had been an asset in college, a useful talent at work, but my always-racing, always-analyzing mind had pushed me to a nervous breakdown five years before. Thin blades of sunlight shining through the not-quite-closed blinds on the east-facing window meant late morning, somewhere around eleven o'clock. Not that the hour mattered; I only worked one day a month, when I made my regular pilgrimage to Atlantic City to win my monthly expenses at the gambling tables. Sometimes it helps to remember every-thing . . . like the number of aces and face-cards played from an eight-deck blackjack shoe.

I had left my silver-handled walking stick leaning up against my night table. Using it, I limped into the kitchen. Four aspirin and a glass of orange juice made breakfast. Then I returned to my bedroom, where I dressed methodically in my last pair of clean Dockers, a blue-and-gold sweater, and worn leather loafers — all remnants from better days, when I had been a *wunderkind* at a Wall Street investment bank. But that had been before my always-racing mind led to a nervous breakdown. And before my run-in with the taxi.

At the front door, I paused just long enough to pull on a Yankees cap and shrug on a windbreaker against the cool October weather. In an act of defiance, I deliberately forgot my toothbrush. Then, taking a firm grip on my walking stick, I slowly limped into the hallway, then out to my building's tiny front porch.

A cold wind gusted, stirring leaves in the gutter. Lowering gray clouds threatened rain. A long black limousine with dark-tinted windows sat double-parked in front of my door, its powerful engine purring. The chauffeur — short but stocky, sporting a military-style haircut and dark sunglasses — opened the rear door and stood stiffly next to it, waiting for me to get in.

Three careful steps down, leaning heavily on the rail, and I reached the sidewalk. When I limped over to the limo, I noticed the bulge of a gun at the chauffeur's right armpit — which meant he was not only armed, but left-handed. Just another useless detail I couldn't help but observe. My mind turned like a well-oiled machine now, noting everything around me and analyzing it.

Surreptitiously, I gave a quick glance up and down the block, but found no sign of life — everybody in my lower working-class neighborhood had already gone off to work or school or whatever else they did during the day: no witnesses left to see my abduction.

Carefully, grimacing a bit, I lowered myself into the extra-roomy back seat and stretched out my legs. They hurt less that way.

Mr. Smith sat inside, dressed — as he had been the last time we met — in an impeccable Italian silk suit. He wore his short salt-and-pepper hair swept back, and the faint scent of lavender surrounded him.

Against my better judgment, I eyed the two glasses in his hands with interest, amber liquid with faintly clinking cubes of ice. As the chauffeur closed the door firmly behind me, Smith passed me a drink. I gulped without hesitation, then made a face. Ginger ale.

'You spoiled perfectly good ice,' I muttered.

'Alcohol kills brain cells, Pit. I want you at your best.'

'Why?' I asked bluntly. My hands started to tremble again. As subtly as I could, I placed the glass into a holder in the door, spilling just a little.

'Because,' he said, 'I have a problem, and you can help me solve it.' It wasn't a request; it was a statement.

Leaning forward, he tapped on the plastic partition separating us from the chauffeur, who had returned to the driver's seat. Slowly we accelerated. At the end of the block, we turned left, heading toward Roosevelt Boulevard.

I half grumbled, 'Why does everyone think I'm some sort of freelance problem-solver?'

'Aren't you?'

'No!'

Smith chuckled again. 'My aunt has a farm west of here. You're going to pay her a visit and keep an eye on things for a week or so. She . . . ' His voice trailed off. I couldn't read anything from his expression. 'Someone — or something — may be stalking her.'

'Some*thing*?' I asked.

'Well . . . ' He shifted a tad uncomfortably. 'She's claimed to see ghosts and angels as long as I can remember.'

'Then she needs a psychiatrist, not a seedy drunken cripple!'

'Come on, Pit! You aren't seedy. Merely depressed.'

'That makes me feel *so* much better,' I grumbled sarcastically. Boy, had my stock fallen. From stopping blackmailers to babysitting crazy aunts.

'Actually,' he went on, 'I sent a couple of my boys out to visit her a month ago. They scared off a prowler one night — though I suppose it might have been a dog or even a coyote. It was dark; they couldn't tell. Anyway, after that, things got quiet. As soon as they left, though, Aunt Peck started reporting disturbances again.'

I frowned. 'What sort of disturbances?'

'Oh . . . noises at night, her possessions disappearing or moving around inside the house. That sort of thing. She thinks the spirit-world is trying to communicate with her.'

'What about you?' I asked. 'Do you believe in these spirits?'

His eyes narrowed. 'Let's say . . . I have an open mind. I've seen a lot of odd things over the years. And believe it or not, I used to be a choirboy. Growing up in the Catholic Church, you get a good strong dose of saints and miracles and superstition.'

I snorted.

'You don't believe?' he asked.

'There are no ghosts, ghouls, zombies, vampires, werewolves, or angels prancing around farms in rural Pennsylvania!' I said it with absolute certainty.

'Then prove it!'

I looked out the window at the passing row houses. Laundry hung outside on tattered lines. Trash and graffiti spoke of a neighborhood heading downhill fast, just like my life. Suddenly I felt old and tired.

Angels . . .

Once upon a time, before my accident, so long ago it felt like someone else's life — once upon a time, when I was a good little boy, I had believed. But now . . .

Frowning, I took a deep breath and slowly let it out. Did I really want to do this? Did I really want to babysit a delusional old lady?

It wasn't like Smith had given me a choice in the matter; we were already on the road, so I might as well make the best of it. Besides, maybe a change of scenery would be good. At least it would keep me from drinking myself to death for a little while longer.

Leaning back, I closed my eyes. 'Tell me,' I said, 'everything you know about your aunt. Start with her name and family background.'

'Don't you want to know about the disturbances?'

'No. You're a second-hand source of

information. If I need to, I'll question her about them.'

'Then you're going?'

My mind was racing ahead. Ghosts . . . farms . . . noises in the night . . .

I sighed. I shook my head.

But I said, 'Yes.'

★ ★ ★

Her name, said Smith, was Elizabeth Peck. She was his mother's sister-in-law: not a blood relative, but marriage meant a lot to his family. As long as he could remember, she had espoused the beneficial effects of fresh air and sunshine on children, and the Pecks' farm — a hundred or so acres just outside Hellersville — played host to a steady stream of young relatives throughout the 1960s and 1970s.

Her husband Joshua had been a lay minister, so the country visits came with generous helpings of sermons . . . especially to the Tortelli boys, the black sheep of the family.

After Uncle Peck's death two years ago,

Aunt Peck began renting her land to neighbors, who planted soybeans, corn, and other crops. She made enough to pay her rather modest bills.

Aunt Peck had always been an avid correspondent, and she still kept in touch with all branches of her extended family through frequent letters. Her speculations about the nightly disturbances being caused by 'angels' had alarmed Smith enough to send a couple of his men out to visit her.

Their first night on the farm, moaning sounds awakened them just after midnight. They ran outside, fired a couple of warning shots into the air, and heard someone — or something — run off through a cornfield. They gave chase, but whoever or whatever it was got away.

Then things got quiet. After another week, they left.

A few days later, Aunt Peck proudly wrote that the 'angels' had returned. Hence Pit's summons.

*   *   *

'She may just be a crazy old lady,' Smith said thoughtfully, 'but she's my aunt, and I have to look out for her. Family duty, you understand.'

Actually, I didn't. My parents were long dead, and I had never been close to any of my other relatives. Uncle Mark's response to my taxi accident had been to send a 'get well soon' card. And he forgot to sign it.

'I'm not sure,' I said, 'whether to be flattered or insulted.'

'Flattered. You're my big gun, Pit.'

I snorted. 'Now you're being silly. But I can't go — I didn't pack my toothbrush, let alone a change of clothes. You'll have to take me home first.'

'Nonsense. I know you don't take instructions well, so I took the liberty of having bags packed for you. Here.'

Reaching into his pocket, he produced a set of miniature steel keys, the kind that fit suitcase locks. The tag dangling from the ring said, 'My Other Car is a BMW.'

'I didn't notice anything missing from my apartment,' I said.

Mentally, I ran through the contents of

my closet and sock drawer as I had seen them this morning. Everything had been exactly where it belonged.

'I purchased a new wardrobe for you, one better suited for farm life.'

My eyebrows raised. 'Oh?'

'Seven flannel shirts of assorted colors; seven black and one white undershirts; seven pairs of blue jeans, waist 28, inseam 30; one Sunday go-to-church suit, from your usual tailor — '

'I don't have a tailor, usual or otherwise,' I said.

He tsk-tsked. 'Perhaps you've forgotten your account at Paolo Versacci's, on Vine Street.' That was where I had bought an Armani suit before visiting his illegal gambling club. 'You made quite an impression on Paolo. He still has your measurements on file.'

It seemed Smith's research on me had been even more complete than I'd thought.

'One purchase does not make him my tailor,' I grumbled. 'Besides, I don't wear flannel. Or jeans. I find them too heavy and binding. And I don't believe in churches, so I won't need a Sunday suit.'

'Show some flexibility.'

'I don't have to. I'm a cripple, remember.'

'That doesn't cut it. We run an equal-opportunity underworld these days, Pit. View your clothes as part of the job — a disguise, if you will. You'll need to blend in on the farm.' Smith took a deep breath, then continued his inventory: 'Heavy wool socks, underwear, light boots, windbreaker, baseball cap, pajamas, and of course a shaving kit, complete with — you guessed it — a toothbrush.'

'You seem to have thought of everything.'

'Of course.'

'Then how are you going to explain me to your aunt?'

I glimpsed a predator's teeth when he smiled. 'We have a charity program at work, helping needy handicapped individuals rehabilitate themselves through clean air and sunshine. She's looking forward to your visit. And, of course, to the $25 *per diem* my company is paying for your room and board.'

'You're too generous,' I said sarcastically. 'But I suppose anything more than that would have aroused her suspicions.'

'Precisely. If she thought I sent you merely to give her some extra money, she never would have agreed.'

Our car took the King of Prussia exit. I leaned forward, eying the landmarks. Lots of new buildings had appeared since the last time I had been here, some ten years before, back when I was a healthy college student.

Smith said, 'You haven't asked what the job pays.'

'It pays something?' Money had been the last thing on my mind.

'A hundred dollars a day, plus reimbursement for any expenses. That's yours just for showing up and keeping my aunt company for a week or two, no matter what happens.'

'I don't want your money.'

'But you'll take it.'

'Do I have a choice?'

He smiled thinly and did not reply.

A few minutes later, we took an exit ramp, then turned into a gas station. Leaning forward slightly, I studied the limo's dashboard. The gas gauge showed nearly full. We weren't here to fuel up.

'This is my stop.' Smith swung open his door. 'I have businesses to run. And *you* have another two-and-a-half hours' drive ahead. Enjoy Hellersville . . . or, as my brothers and I used to call it, Hell!'

He slid out, and without preamble my chauffeur pulled into traffic and accelerated again. When I glanced over my shoulder, Smith raised two fingers to his forehead in salute. Then a new Burger King hid him from view.

★ ★ ★

Ten minutes later, we were on the Pennsylvania Turnpike heading west, surrounded by pleasantly monotonous trees and the occasional sprawling farm, complete with picture-perfect horses and cows. Traffic remained light. Little here could stimulate my over-active mind; I found it soothing.

With nothing better to do, I closed my eyes and tried to sleep. Flannel shirts . . . blue jeans . . . fresh air and sunshine . . . Hell indeed for a city boy like me.

What had I gotten myself into?

When the rhythm of the car abruptly changed, I jolted awake. We had taken an exit ramp.

According to the clock in the dashboard up front, almost three hours had passed since we left King of Prussia. The afternoon sunlight seemed too crisp, the rumble of wheels on pavement too sharp. My stomach growled faintly. Rubbing crusty-feeling eyes, I longed for a stiff drink. I had to press my hands against my thighs to keep them from shaking uncontrollably. God, I wanted to go home.

At the toll booth, the driver paid cash. Then we sped down a rural highway. Two turns later, we were on a narrow country road. Fields to either side had just been harvested, leaving a rough stubble of cut-down cornstalks. A pair of huge red harvesting machines sat idle.

As we drove, farm complexes broke the fields every half mile or so: old houses, ancient barns, silos, sheds, dogs and horses and the occasional cow or sheep. At least they had garbage pickup; at the end of each driveway sat identical green plastic bins stenciled 'Waste Management.' A few driveways had bonus items out: a threadbare sectional sofa, a rusted old bicycle, piles of broken-down cardboard boxes neatly tied into bundles.

Then we turned onto a gravel driveway. In crooked letters, the battered metal mailbox said PECK — 2040.

We had arrived. I sat up straighter, studying a large old barn with peeling red paint, three ancient silver silos, and a sprawling Victorian-style farmhouse that had seen better days. A clothesline running between ancient oaks held faded yellow sheets. To the left of the house, in a chicken-wired pen, fifteen chickens scratched and strutted.

My chauffeur pulled up beside a pink Cadillac twenty years out of style, honked twice, then cut the engine. Immediately a plump, cheery-faced woman in a red-and-white checked dress burst from the house. She wore her gray hair up in a tight bun, and a smudge of white — flour? — dotted the tip of her nose. She had that pleasant, beaming expression I had always associated with grandmothers, and half against my will I found myself smiling back.

The chauffeur opened the door for me. I fumbled with my walking stick for a moment, then climbed out awkwardly.

'Hello!' I said through clenched teeth. I tried for a happy note, but it came out as a desperate croak. I had been sitting in one position too long; fierce stabbing pains shot the length of my legs.

'Hello yourself!' she replied. I tried not to wince; she spoke at full volume. 'Call me Aunt Peck — everyone does. You must be Mr. Geller? Pete? Petey?'

'My friends call me Pit, Aunt Peck.' Not that I had any left, but Pit was several steps better than Petey.

'Lord above, what an interesting name! You must have quite a story to tell about it!'

'Not really — ' I began.

She swept past me, all but bouncing with energy and enthusiasm. The chauffeur had opened the trunk. Without hesitation, Aunt Peck seized a blue leather suitcase and a matching garment bag, then started for the house.

'Come on, Pit!' she called over her

69

shoulder. 'I've got pies in the oven! Can't let 'em burn!'

I looked at the chauffeur. 'I suppose it's too late to back out?'

'Sorry, pal,' he said. 'Orders.'

I nodded. You didn't contradict a man like Mr. Smith. Leaning heavily on my walking stick, I limped after Aunt Peck.

★　★　★

She was a talker — I'll say that much for her. As I sat at the kitchen table and worked on a slab of hot-from-the-oven apple pie topped with freshly whipped cream, she kept up a nonstop monologue about everything under the sun *except* angelic visitors — the farm, her late husband Joshua, the city kids who had just moved in next door.

'City kids?' I prompted. New neighbors explained all the cardboard boxes out for trash pickup.

'Nick and Debby,' she said. 'You'll meet them tomorrow. I always invite neighbors over for Saturday dinner. It makes things

70

a little less lonely. Of course, now that you're here . . . '

I nodded encouragingly. 'Have they been here long — Nick and Debby?'

'Oh, a bit over a month, I guess. Maybe two.'

'Ah.' I ate my last bite of pie. My hands kept shaking, but Aunt Peck either didn't notice or marked it down to my accident.

How closely did the new neighbors' arrival coincide with the disturbances? Could they be trying to scare her off her land? Pennsylvania had its share of natural resources . . . what could make her land valuable enough to steal? Oil, perhaps?

'I was wondering,' I said, wiping my mouth carefully on a napkin, 'if you have well water?'

'Of course. Why?'

'In the late 1800s, my many-times great-grandfather had a farm in Pennsylvania. He gave up on it and moved to Ohio because every time he tried to dig a well, it filled up with black oily stuff.'

She laughed; everyone who heard it always did. According to family legend,

71

it had really happened. And Marilyn Monroe used to baby-sit my father and uncle, too, before she got famous.

Aunt Peck said, 'I bet your family has been kicking themselves ever since automobiles came along!'

'Yes.' I shook my head ruefully. 'I guess you don't have that problem here, though.'

'Oil companies poked around in '75 or '76, doing all sorts of surveys, but apparently there's nothing under Hellersville but water.'

Strike one theory.

'Surely the town has *something* going for it . . . ' I said. 'Mines? Silver? Gold?'

'Well . . . there used to be a quarry. They made gravel, I think — but then it filled with water. It's been a lake for nearly fifty years now. All Hellersville produces *is* produce.' She gave a wink. 'But wait till you taste my tomatoes — they're as big as softballs and sweet as anything! And my watermelons!' She laughed heartily.

Strike a second theory. If the land had no intrinsic value, why would anyone want to scare her off her farm?

After I finished my pie, Aunt Peck offered to show me my room. She retrieved my bags from the hallway, where she had left them while we checked her pies, then skirted the narrow stairs (which I had been dreading) and headed down a wide hallway. The floorboards creaked loudly as we walked: no one would be able to sneak up on us during the night.

We reached a cluttered family room. The sofa, wing-backed chairs, and ottoman all had plastic over the upholstery. Books, curios, and photos crammed the built-in shelves and the standalone bookcases. A small TV sat next to the fi replace.

We passed through into another small hallway, then came to a small bedroom at the back of the house. It had one window, which looked out across fields stubbled from recently harvested corn. To the left, I saw the edge of her garden — tomato and pepper plants.

I nodded approvingly at the single bed with a white quilt and two fluffy pillows. It looked a lot like my bed back in

Philadelphia. A threadbare oval rug, made of tiny triangles of randomly chosen fabric set in a spiral pattern, covered much of the floor. An oak dresser and a battered old armoire completed the furnishings.

As she set the bags on the bed, I straightened the pictures on the walls: three faded black-and-white photographs showing children standing in army-like formations before this same farmhouse. Smiling girls wore knee-length dresses with bows in their hair; boys wore short pants and shirts with buttons, their hair buzzed so close they almost looked bald. The men behind them all wore white shirts with dark ties, and the women wore plain dresses. Dates written in the lower corners said July 13, 1961, July 8, 1962, and July 14, 1963. They had to commemorate the family gatherings Mr. Smith had disliked so much.

That would make Smith one of the boys. I studied their faces, but couldn't pick him out — nearly identical clothes, haircuts, and suntans made him blend in among the others. Smith's father, though, stood out among the men — shorter and darker than the others, leaner, with a somewhat sinister look in his eyes: a younger, rougher version of Mr. Smith.

'You used to have a lot of guests,' I said to Aunt Peck. 'Where did you put them all?'

'Oh, we put the boys in the barn — plenty of room in the hayloft — and the girls slept in the family room. We had six bedrooms upstairs for the adults.'

'I was an only child. It must have been great to have so many family members together.'

'Oh, it was wonderful.' She sighed, eyes distant. 'Those were the days.' Then she brightened. 'Do you want me to unpack your things?'

'No, thank you. I can manage. I try to be self-reliant.'

'My Joshua was the same way, God rest his soul.' She started back for the kitchen. 'I'll start supper. Give a holler if you need anything.'

'Thanks.'

* * *

I spent the next half hour unpacking. Everything Mr. Smith had purchased looked like it would fit me. With careful precision, I opened packages of socks and then refolded the contents, placing each garment neatly and precisely in the dresser drawers. Next I meticulously removed all the tags from my new shirts and hung them in the armoire. Jeans didn't need hangers, so I stacked them in the bottom.

Mindless activities let my racing mind slow down. For a few minutes, I could forget Aunt Peck's problems and concentrate solely on the *here* and *now*.

The last things in the suitcase turned out to be a tiny cell phone and a small but powerful flashlight, batteries already installed. I turned on the phone and checked the list of numbers. Speed-dial had been pre-programmed with several numbers:

Smith 001
Fast help 002

Smith really had thought of everything. I switched it off and put both phone and flashlight in the front of my sock drawer.

Next I opened the garment bag. My new suit turned out to be a Joseph Abboud original, gray with pinstripes, 100% wool: practical and conservative enough not to stand out in a rural farming community. Mr. Smith had good taste, if nothing else. I hung it up, then put my bags on top of the armoire. I made one last pass over the room, straightening the dresser slightly, lowering the shade so it covered the window latch, and picking a few bits of lint from the bed's white quilt.

Lastly, I opened the window and peered out. Now I could see the whole of Aunt Peck's garden, and I had to admit it was impressive: a rectangle perhaps thirty feet long and sixty wide, enclosed with chicken wire and planted with peppers, tomatoes, pumpkins, and quite a few other vegetables I couldn't identify at this distance. Other than the garden and a couple of shade trees, the land around the farmhouse had been cleared for more than two hundred yards in every direction. Nobody could sneak up on the house — or, having gotten here, escape unseen the way the last prowler had.

I made my way back toward the kitchen, straightening pictures along the way, examining rooms with greater attention. The books in the family room seemed to be a mix of espionage novels and religious nonfiction. Family photos showed Aunt Peck and a man I took to be Joshua with five children and in a variety of settings, from Disneyworld to Hershey Park. I committed the position of every item in every room to memory. If these alleged angels moved or made off with anything, I would notice.

The plastic covers on the sofa and chairs had tiny pinprick indentations — probably cat claws, since cat hair in several different colors speckled the throw pillows.

Then, as I made my way toward the kitchen, I heard voices. Visitors? I strained to hear, but couldn't make out the words.

As quietly as I could, I crept up the hallway and peeked around the corner. Aunt Peck had her back to me as she stirred something on the stove — soup or stew, from the smell. An old man in coveralls sat at the kitchen table nursing a mug of coffee. He looked at least seventy, maybe older: thinning white hair, weather-beaten skin, rough calloused hands.

' — ought to be ripped out and replaced,' he was saying. 'Wouldn't take more'n a day or two, and you wouldn't have to worry about the termite damage. Can't have you fallin' through the floor.'

'I don't have the money right now,' said Aunt Peck. 'It will have to wait.'

As his fingers curled tightly around his white coffee mug, I noticed that the little finger and ring finger of his right hand were both missing their last joints.

'Wouldn't cost more'n a couple hundred for lumber, Bessie. A wise investment, if you ask me. Happy to throw in the labor for free, just to keep you safe.'

'Maybe next year.'

'Suit yourself. But the damage ain't goin' to go away.'

'I know, Joe.' She sighed. 'But my heart just isn't into keeping things up anymore. Joshua used to handle all that.'

Joe frowned. 'You do what you can,

Bessie. You do what you can.'

He drained his mug and shoved back his chair. 'I better get goin'. My boy and I can fix the barn tomorrow afternoon. Just needs a few new shingles, and I have plenty at home.'

'Thanks, Joe.'

Then, to my shock, she gave him a kiss — not a casual peck, but a downright passionate smooch — and he returned it heartily, along with a squeeze that made her squeal. Clearly the old folks had some friskiness left inside.

Joe left through the side door, which led into the yard facing the barn. After it slammed shut, I counted to ten, then limped into the kitchen.

'I heard voices,' I said. Through the door's window, I watched Joe climb into a battered blue Ford truck and slowly drive away.

'Joe Carver stopped by.' Aunt Peck nodded as she stirred her pot. 'He's worked on the farm since the day we moved in here. The hardest thing I ever had to do was let him go when Joshua passed. He and his boy still do all the little jobs I can't handle.'

'Ah,' I said. I picked up both coffee mugs and carried them carefully to the sink. Aunt Peck hadn't stirred hers well enough; a thick white residue of sugar remained on the bottom when I poured out the dregs. 'Does he live around here, too?'

'He has a little house in Hellersville. His wife kept it cute as a button till she got sick last spring. This was the first year they didn't plant new flowers.' She shook her head. 'Poor dear. She passed just after Joshua.'

Two old friends who had lost their spouses. No wonder they felt drawn to each other.

*   *   *

At dinner, my hands shook so badly I could barely eat. I spilled all the water from my glass twice, soaking myself and the table. I apologized profusely as I wiped at everything with my napkin.

'Land sakes, it's just water, Pit!' said Aunt Peck with a laugh. She fetched a towel from the kitchen and mopped up. 'After five babies and Joshua's passing, a little spilled water isn't going to bother me!'

'You're very kind,' I said miserably. *Stop shaking, stop shaking!* I pressed both hands together in my lap, but it didn't help. My body wouldn't cooperate. What I needed was a drink. Did Joshua keep a supply of booze in the house? Probably not; he had been a minister, after all.

Aunt Peck returned to her seat and began to eat her stew again — a thick one full of beef, carrots, and potatoes, just the way I liked it.

'You must be wondering what happened to me,' I said as I struggled with my fork. With effort, I managed to spear a carrot and get it into my mouth without impaling myself.

'Do you feel like talking about it . . . ?'

'I don't mind.' I half shrugged and put my fork down. Eating wasn't worth the effort tonight. 'I used to work on Wall Street. I got a plum job right out of college, but I had a nervous breakdown from working twenty-hour days seven days a week. After six months of treatment, when I finally began to pull myself together again, a taxi ran a red light and hit me. I spent an hour pinned under its front wheels, and I almost lost my legs. I spent another six months in rehab . . . and I just haven't been the same since.'

'I'm so sorry, Pit.' She touched my hand gently. 'I'll pray for you.'

I didn't particularly want her sympathy — what's done is done; no use crying over it or hoping for miracles that would never come — but she said it in such a heartfelt way that I couldn't help but feel touched.

'Thank you,' I said.

*　*　*

After dinner, she invited me to watch game shows with her, and to my surprise I accepted. I used to find game shows annoying and contrived. But now, tonight, it was almost . . . *comforting* . . . to have someone with whom I could sit in silence . . . someone who made no demands on my intellect or time or will to live.

Jeopardy had three really bad contestants; even the returning champion flubbed answer after answer. The host, struggling to put a positive spin on things, quipped that tonight's questions must be harder than usual.

'That's not the problem, Alex,' I couldn't help but blurt out. 'You picked idiots to play.'

'Can you do better?' Aunt Peck asked with a yawn. I think she had been watching me more than the television.

'It's always easier when you're at home.' I forced a laugh. But then I proceeded to come up with questions for every single answer on *Jeopardy* — and for the final answer, I came up with not just two, but all seven members of the United Arab Emirates. None of the players got it right. The least unskillful of the three — or perhaps the most cunning — had only risked a dollar and won the day, complete with a laughably small $1,200 jackpot.

'That was amazing, Pit!' Aunt Peck said, staring at me in awe. 'You should go on TV. You'd win a fortune!'

'I don't think I can stand long enough to play. And besides, I don't like to travel. It took a lot of arm-twisting to get me out here!'

'I imagine Cal can be quite persuasive.' She smiled wistfully, eyes distant, remembering. 'The Tortellis were always that way.'

'Cal is . . . quite something.' How much did she know about him? Somehow, I suspected she had no idea he ran an illegal casino.

'Oh, Cal's a kitten. Best of the lot. Be glad you never met his father. There was a man who . . . well, I shouldn't speak ill of the dead.' She paused. 'But when Bruno wanted something, he got it — no matter what.'

'Was he in organized crime?'

'What makes you ask that?' she said sharply.

'Something Cal once said.'

'I don't know for sure — he kept his business to himself, at least around me — but Joshua always said he was some sort of gangster. When the police found him dead in the trunk of a car, that clinched it for us.'

'How long ago did that happen?'

'Well, let's see . . . it must have been 1963 — early August, I think. He had been shot with a single bullet to the head.'

'It must have been hard on his family,' I said. To my surprise, I found I had a lump in my throat. I remembered my own father's death from pancreatic cancer. It had been devastating to Mom and me; she had never recovered from it.

'Yes. Yes, it was. But the Lord gives and the Lord takes — maybe it was for the best. At least Cal and the other boys didn't follow their father into a life of crime, so something good came of it.'

She yawned, covering her mouth with a plump-fingered hand. 'Oh, excuse me!'

'Quite all right. I'm tired, too.' Farm people went to bed early, I reminded myself. 'If you don't mind, I think I'll turn in.'

'Me too.' She yawned again, then stood unsteadily. I reached up and steadied her arm. 'I can barely keep my eyes open!'

★ ★ ★

Once Aunt Peck disappeared up the stairs, I prowled through the house, doing a quick security check. She had left all three outside doors unlocked, so I locked them. None had deadbolts or chains, unfortunately; they all should have been replaced with steel-core security doors years ago. The basement door had a simple hook and eye; nothing I could do about it now, so I left it alone.

Next, I examined all the windows. Not one single lock had been turned, so I did it myself. Perhaps they didn't believe in burglars out here. Or perhaps they didn't have much worth stealing.

Returning to my bedroom, I opened my window about three inches. A cool wind began to billow the curtains. If angels or ghosts wanted in tonight, they would have to get past me.

I did not undress. Instead, I lay on top of the quilt, listening to the unfamiliar noises around me. Houses have their own rhythms: the creaks, the squeaks, the little settling sounds. When the furnace suddenly kicked on with a *whump*, I jumped so much, I almost fell out of bed.

A little later, raccoons or possums or some other beasts I had never heard before began to yowl and hiss in the yard. Mating? Fighting? Slaughtering the chickens? I had no way of knowing. Since Aunt Peck didn't come running down from her bedroom in a panic, I assumed the racket fell into the 'typical farm sound' category.

Then I heard a low but steady *crunch-crunch-crunch*: tires on gravel. The vehicle was moving very, very slowly toward the house.

Rising as fast as I could, I grabbed my phone and flashlight and went down the creaking hallway, through the family room, and into the parlor, just to the right of the front door. Peering around the drapes, I gazed into the front yard. A large, dark vehicle rolled up to the house and glided to a stop: no headlights showed, and when the driver opened the door, no cab light came on. Could this be Aunt Peck's angel?

The driver went around back and got

something out of the bed of his truck, then carried it toward the house. The breath caught in my throat as heavy footsteps sounded on the steps, then the porch.

I hobbled around to the front door and flipped all the switches on the wall. The porch and the hallway flooded with light. Through the little window set in the front door, I saw Joe Carver's startled face, then heard a metallic crash as he dropped something heavy.

'Bessie?' he called. He tried the door handle, but it was locked. He jiggled it.

'What are you doing here?' I demanded.

'Who are you?' he called. Rather than run away, as I'd half expected, he began to pound on the door. 'Bessie? Are you okay in there? Open up!'

'Stop that!' I said.

'Open up!' he shouted. 'Bessie? Bessie?'

Those weren't the actions of a prowler. I fumbled with the lock and opened the door.

'Who the hell are you?' Joe demanded, staring at me. The loud crashing noise had been his toolkit — he had dropped it when I turned on the lights.

'I'm Peter Geller,' I said, leaning heavily on my walking stick. 'I'm visiting Aunt Peck for the week. Now who the hell are *you?*'

Joe looked me up and down. I guess I didn't strike him as dangerous or threatening — me, thin as a rail, eyes limned with dark circles, looking closer to sixty than my true age of thirty — because he didn't try to tear me to pieces. Which he probably could have done with very little effort.

'You one of her nephews?' he demanded. He took a step forward, face cycling through anger and puzzlement. 'She didn't say nothing about you comin'.'

'It must have slipped her mind,' I said. 'She didn't say anything about expecting burglars, either!'

'I'm not a burglar!'

'You could have fooled me, sneaking around like that!'

His fists balled up; he seemed about to take my head off. I shifted uneasily. Maybe I had chosen the wrong approach. He wasn't responding well to confrontation.

'Say,' I said, pretending to study his features. Time to change tactics — and fast. 'Don't I know you? You're Joe Carver, right?'

'Huh.' He squinted hard at my face, but seemed to draw a blank. 'How do you know me?'

'We met years ago,' I lied. 'I was just a kid, and I didn't have *this*.' I raised my walking stick.

'Huh,' he said again.

I peered around him at his truck. 'I heard you come up the drive, but your headlights were off. That's why I thought you were a burglar.'

'I was trying not to wake Bessie,' he said. He frowned. 'Termites been eatin' into the dinin' room floor. I need to replace it or she's gonna fall through and break a leg. Maybe worse. She wouldn't let me do it, so I thought I'd come by tonight and get started. Once the floor's up, she'll have to let me finish.'

He had the lines down so well, he must have practiced them. Smiling, I swung the front door fully open.

'Come in, Mr. Carver. I'm sorry if I

was rude — but you scared the bejesus out of me. I wasn't expecting anyone. And you have to admit a cripple like me can't exactly defend the house. You understand.'

'Uh-huh.'

I glanced over my shoulder at the stairs, brow furrowing. 'And I'm surprised Aunt Peck's not up, considering all the racket we've made.'

'Bessie sleeps like a log.' He said it a little too fast. 'Don't fret yourself about her. Early to bed, early to rise.'

Mental alarms went off. Hard work and country air might make someone tired. But nobody could have slept through the crash of his dropped toolbox or the shouting we'd done at each other. No, Aunt Peck should have been down here in a flash to investigate.

Then I remembered the white sludge in the bottom of her coffee mug. I had taken it for sugar. But it could have been something else — some drug to make her sleep, so Joe could get in here and do . . . what? Haunt the place?

'Well, at least *someone*'s tired,' I said

with a chuckle. I had to put him at ease and get away long enough to check on Aunt Peck. 'I'm going to have to take my pain pills to get to sleep tonight.'

'Yeah,' he said. 'You should do that.'

I nodded and smiled. 'If you don't mind, I'm going to turn in. Good night, Mr. Carver.'

'Good night.' He picked up his toolbox, then pushed past me into the dining room.

I limped with deliberate noisiness down the hallway — a shuffling step, then a tap of my walking stick, then another shuffling step, then another tap, floorboards creaking underfoot all the time. Halfway to my room, I heard a slight noise behind me, and I could feel his eyes following my every move. Hopefully he found my performance convincing.

Without a backward glance, I entered my room and shut the door. Then, so slowly it hurt, I counted to a hundred. When I peeked out, he had gone back to doing whatever mischief he had come to do.

I pulled out my cell phone and flipped

it open. Number 002 on the speed dial list still said, 'Fast help.' But what did that mean — police? FBI? Mob hit-men? I needed muscle, and I needed it fast. Despite his affection for Aunt Peck, I didn't exactly feel safe with Joe in the house.

Taking a deep breath, I pushed button 2. On the first ring, a man picked up and said in a gravely voice, 'Smith's office.'

'This is Peter Geller. I need someone here. Fast.'

'Five minutes,' he said and hung up.

Five minutes. I could last that long.

Slowly I eased myself out into the hallway, closed the door silently behind me, and crept up the hallway toward the narrow stairs. I placed my feet as close to the wall as I could, hoping the floorboards wouldn't squeak. Tiptoeing along that way, without using my walking stick really hurt; I put too much weight on the balls of my feet, and the shooting pains it caused brought tears to my eyes.

But it worked. The floorboards remained silent.

When I passed the door to the dining

room, Joe had his back to me. He had rolled up half the rug and was examining the floorboards. Looking for termite damage? Somehow, I doubted it.

I reached the staircase. Cautiously, I placed my foot on the first step. The stairs had barely squeaked when Aunt Peck went up them at bedtime. I estimated my own weight at seventy to eighty pounds less than hers, so I anticipated little trouble. Grasping the railing, I hauled myself up an inch at a time. Three steps, and not a sound; six steps, halfway there; eight steps, and I knew I'd make it.

I paused at the top landing. The door to Aunt Peck's room stood open. Dim light spilled in from the hallway, and I could just make out her queen-sized bed and several bulky pieces of furniture. I flipped on the overhead lights and went in.

She lay on top of her quilt, still wearing that red-and-white checked dress; she hadn't had a chance to put on her nightgown — she had just collapsed, unconscious or dead.

'Aunt Peck?' I called softly.

From below, ancient nails groaned as they pulled free from a board. By the sounds, Joe hadn't been lying: he really *was* pulling up the floor.

'Aunt Peck?' I called again, louder.

When she still didn't respond, I limped over and shook her shoulder. Nothing. Her forehead glistened faintly with perspiration; when I touched her carotid artery, she had a fast, fluttery heartbeat. Drugged?

No more than two or three minutes had passed since I'd called Smith's office for help. How fast would Hellerville's EMS respond to a 911 call? Who would get here first?

Taking a deep breath, I dialed 911. I couldn't risk an old woman's life.

'Emergency services,' said a tinny voice.

'I need an ambulance,' I said.

'What is the nature of your emergency?'

'I have an old woman here who's unconscious. Possible drug overdose. I don't know what she took.'

'What is your location?'

I gave the address. 'How long will it take to get someone here?'

'I have already alerted the police, sir. They should arrive shortly. Can you remain on the line?'

Behind me, I heard a voice say, 'What are you doing?'

A chill swept through me. I whirled — and found Joe Carver silhouetted in the doorway. With two quick strides, he reached me and ripped the cell phone from my hand.

'Aunt Peck — ' I began.

'You leave her be!' He raised his fist to strike me, face drawing back in rage.

Then the doorbell rang. A second later someone began to pound on the door. The cavalry had arrived. Far off, I heard the wail of an ambulance's siren.

Joe hesitated, then lowered his fist. He looked over his shoulder, clearly uneasy.

'The police are here,' I said in a soothing voice. 'You better run down and let them in. I think Aunt Peck had a stroke.'

'A — a stroke?' He gaped at me.

'Please — let them in!' I let a note of

urgency creep into my voice. 'We have to get her to a hospital!'

The cell phone in his hand began to ring. I reached out and plucked it from his fingers.

'Go!' I said, pointing at the stairs. 'Let them in!'

He turned and thundered down the steps. I heard him babbling to the police about how poor old Bessie must have had a stroke, how they needed to get her to a hospital.

Then I answered the cell phone: 'Peter Geller.'

'You've got cops there,' said the man with the gravelly voice. 'We drove past. What do you want me to do?'

'Circle around. Come in quietly as soon as they're gone.'

'Anything else?'

'Call Smith and tell him to get out here fast. It's important.'

'Got it.' He hung up.

I stuck the phone in my pocket as two uniformed police officers came bounding up the stairs carrying medical cases. Both cops looked young — maybe twenty-three or twenty-four, with close-shaved heads and plenty of muscles bulging beneath their uniforms. One started taking Aunt Peck's blood pressure while the other did a circuit of the room, scooping vials of pills from her dresser into a plastic bag.

'You phoned it in?' the cop asked me. Pulling out a stethoscope and a blood pressure cuff, he started to take Aunt Peck's blood pressure. 'Do you know what's wrong with her?'

Over his shoulder, I read Aunt Peck's blood pressure: 160 over 90. Much too high.

'Yes, I know what's wrong.' My gaze flickered over to Joe Carver, standing in the doorway wringing his hands. 'It's a drug overdose.'

'Why do you think so?'

'I noticed a white residue in her coffee mug. I think there were pills in it.'

'A — a stroke!' Joe said. His face had gone bone white. 'You said it was a stroke!'

'No, it wasn't a stroke.'

'Where is the coffee mug?' the first cop asked.

'She washed it.'

The second cop said, 'Besides the ones here, do you know of any other pills she might have taken?'

'No.' Again I looked at Joe, but he volunteered nothing.

The ambulance's siren cut off as it pulled into the farm's driveway; I could see its flashing lights through the drawn shades. The police officer who had collected the pills pushed past Joe and jogged down the stairs to show them in.

Two minutes later, they had Aunt Peck on a stretcher and carried her down. All the fuss and attention seemed to have finally penetrated her stupor. She half opened her eyes and looked at me.

'Angels . . . ' she whispered.

Maybe that's where all her visitations had come from — drug-induced dreams. Which meant Joe had dosed her before. All the pieces of the puzzle were falling neatly into place. Everything except *why*.

When I patted her arm gently, she closed her eyes and went back to sleep.

'Where will they take her?' I asked the police.

'County hospital,' the first officer said. 'It's the closest. Don't worry, they'll take good care of her.'

'I should go, too,' muttered Joe. 'Bessie . . . '

'No,' I said firmly. 'You aren't family. The hospital won't let you in.' Pointedly, I added, 'Besides, you've done quite enough for Aunt Peck already.'

Joe stared at me, eyes glittering with hatred. 'Then *you* should go.'

'I'd love to, but I'm not family, either.'

'But you said — '

I smiled sweetly. 'I lied.'

Just then the first police officer returned and asked for my name. I told him the truth, and he wrote it down. Then he did the same to Joe. A little sullenly, Joe told him.

Joe and I stood side by side on the front porch, watching in silence as first the ambulance and then the police car peeled away — the ambulance with its lights flashing, the police car dark but close behind.

'I ought to kill you,' Joe Carver announced.

'That would not be wise.' I shifted

uncomfortably, leaning heavily on my walking stick. 'We're about to have company. Very powerful and very *mean* company who won't like what you did to Aunt Peck. And then we're going to find the money.'

It was a stab in the dark, but his response told me I'd guessed right.

'How do you know about the money — ' he gasped out.

'I work for Bruno Tortelli's son.'

Joe sagged, all the fight gone out of him. He sat on the porch steps and began to sob quietly.

Just as he managed to compose himself, a black car pulled into the driveway, tires crunching on the gravel. It parked beside the pink Cadillac, and two stocky men in dark suits climbed out. Both carried hand-guns in shoulder holsters.

'Mr. Geller?' asked the driver.

'That's me,' I said. 'Is Mr. Smith coming?'

'Yes.'

'Excellent.' I turned and limped toward the front door. 'Let's wait inside. My feet are killing me. Oh, and don't let Mr. Carver leave.'

The mantle clock showed 3:10 when I heard another car pull up in the yard. One of the guards got up to check. He returned a moment later with Mr. Smith.

'This had better be good,' Smith said even before I'd managed to pull myself to my feet. He looked tired and rumpled and unhappy at being dragged out here.

'I think you'll be pleased,' I said.

He folded his arms. 'Proceed.'

'Surely you remember Joe Carver from your childhood days here.' I indicated Joe with a nod of my head.

Smith frowned. 'The handyman?'

'Correct. But this story starts in 1963. Your father stole some money and brought it out here. Somehow, he talked Reverend Peck into holding onto it for him — together, they hid it inside the house. I believe Joe can corroborate that part of the story. Joe?'

'Yeah,' Joe said sullenly. 'That's what happened.'

'Unfortunately,' I went on, 'your father was killed before he could return for it.

And Reverend Peck refused to touch the money because it was stolen.'

'Go on,' said Smith, looking interested.

I said, 'Decades passed. Somehow, Joe heard about the money — '

'Joshua was dyin',' said Joe Carver. 'Out of his head, just babblin'. He thought I was Bruno Tortelli, and he began arguin' with me. Said he couldn't keep the money here. Said he wanted it gone before Bessie found out.'

I continued, 'So that's when Joe decided to take the money for himself. His wife died sick — it probably left him deep in debt. He wanted to clear himself so he could remarry. I'm sure he had the best motives.'

'Where does my aunt fit into this?' Mr. Smith asked.

'She doesn't believe in locking doors or windows,' I said. 'Joe has been coming at night and searching for the money. She attributed the noises and disturbances to ghosts and angels. But Joe couldn't find the money. Now he thinks it may be hidden under the floorboards. This afternoon, he drugged your aunt — probably with one of the medicines his wife used to take — and he came out tonight planning to rip up the floorboards.'

Smith looked around. 'Where *is* Aunt Peck?'

'In the hospital. I found her drugged, so I called an ambulance. She's a strong old girl; she'll be fine.'

'She better be.' Smith gave Joe a dark look. 'If anything happens to her . . . '

'Right now,' I said, 'I think we should look for the money. I'm willing to bet Joe got it right. It's under the floor. But not in the dining room.'

'Where, then?' said Joe.

'Did you notice,' I said to Joe, 'that the steps to the second floor don't squeak?'

'No. But what of it?'

'In a house this old, the steps *should* squeak. All the other floorboards do. I think someone took the staircase apart and put it back together more firmly. And someone has been giving the steps extra attention over the years to keep them in tiptop shape.'

'All this time . . . ' Joe muttered. 'All this time, and I never even suspected!'

'Of course, I could be wrong.' I pulled myself to my feet. 'Mr. Smith? Shall we have a look?'

'Certainly!'

Joe Carver fetched a crowbar from his toolbox and brought it to the staircase. He hunted around the first step, looking for the right spot, then deftly inserted the thin end of the crowbar and pried.

With a groan, the nails pulled free. Then the step popped up . . . and in a dusty little hole under the first step, I spotted three dusty canvas bags. Each had been stenciled with 'Manhattan Federal Trust' in dark blue letters.

Smith pushed Joe aside, took out the bags, and dumped neat stacks of twenty dollar bills wrapped in paper bands onto the floor. Fifty-five bundles of bills — not so much these days, but in 1963 it would have been a fortune.

Smith tossed me one of the stacks. I flipped through the bills slowly: fifty of them, exactly one thousand dollars.

'The serial numbers are non-sequential,' I observed. 'This money has been circulated. And there are a few gold certificates in here. They may be worth more to collectors than the face value of the bills.' I tossed the bundle back onto the pile. 'Probably safe to spend.'

'Dad knew his stuff,' Mr. Smith said.

'What are we going to do with it?' Joe asked him. 'Divide it up?'

'Return it to its rightful owner,' said Smith.

Of course, he meant himself. But Joe didn't know that.

'Is there a reward?' Joe asked, sounding desperate. He licked his lips. 'Maybe . . . a finder's fee?'

Smith frowned. 'Trying to steal from my aunt was a stupid thing to do. Drugging her was worse. This — ' He sneered at the money. '*This* is nothing. It's hardly worth my time. But to protect my family — my flesh and blood — I would happily give ten times as much.'

He nodded to his men. They grabbed Joe's arms in vice-like grips. Joe yelled in sudden panic as he realized how things had suddenly turned against him.

Smith smiled at me. 'Once again, Pit, I'm impressed. You gave me more than I expected. Now, please wait in my car.

This won't take long.'

I swallowed hard. Suddenly I had a very bad feeling inside.

Carefully, Smith took off his coat, folded it neatly, and set it onto the hall table. Then he removed his cufflinks and slipped them into his pants pocket. Slowly he began to roll up his sleeves.

'You won't kill him,' I said.

'Not as long as my aunt recovers.'

I nodded. I understood — even if Joe didn't. Family came first with Mr. Smith.

'One more thing you should know,' I said.

'What's that?'

'As long as you're keeping it in the family . . . Joe is going to be your uncle. Your aunt is in love with him.'

Then I turned and walked out. Mr. Smith's chauffeur had been waiting for me; he held the door open, and I slid into the back seat to wait.

★   ★   ★

About five minutes later, the two goons came out, looking unhappy. They got into their car and drove away. A few minutes later, Mr. Smith came out. He had put his coat back on. And he didn't look happy.

He got in next to me, then motioned for the driver to proceed. We pulled out of the driveway and headed back for the turnpike. He opened the little compartment with the martini glass on it and poured himself a glass of generic ginger ale.

'Want some, Pit?'

'No.'

He took a long drink. 'You must be wondering,' he finally said, 'what happened inside.'

'I assume you gave him a wedding present,' I said, 'and welcomed him to the family.'

Smith hadn't carried the money out. I would have noticed something that bulky.

'We also set a wedding date,' Mr. Smith said, frowning. 'He has a month to get his affairs in order. And he knows what will happen if he ever steps out of line again.'

I leaned back with a half smile. 'There's still the matter of my fee. For twelve hours' work, you owe me fifty bucks. I'll take it in chips next time I visit your casino.'

'I think,' said Mr. Smith slowly, studying me, 'that you might be the most dangerous man I've ever met, Pit.'

'I'll take that as a compliment,' I said. Then I closed my eyes and tried to go to sleep.

My legs hurt less that way.

3

A Christmas Pit

When my doorbell rang, the sound jolted through me like an electric shock. I accidentally sloshed Jack Daniels across my lap and began cursing all unexpected visitors.

Carefully, so I wouldn't spill another drop, I set the bottle on my night table, grabbed my walking stick, and swung my ruined legs over the side of the bed. Standing usually hurt, but I'd already drunk enough to feel a comfortable numbness instead.

The doorbell rang a second time, an annoying *brzzz* that set my teeth on edge.

'Stop that racket! I'm coming!' I yelled. I shrugged a robe over my underwear, knotting the belt halfheartedly, and limped out into my rather Spartan family room.

By the time I turned the deadbolt and

yanked open the front door, I half expected to find the hallway deserted. The brats upstairs enjoyed playing jokes like that — 'bait the cripple,' I called it.

Tonight, however, I found a soggy young man in an Atlanta Braves baseball cap and a cheap brown coat. Water pooled around him and the duffel bag he'd set down. Rain — that explained why my legs had been aching worse than usual.

'What do you want?' I demanded. 'Don't you know what time it is?'

Involuntarily, he covered his mouth and nose and took a half step back. I had to reek like a distillery.

'Uh . . . six o'clock?' he said. His voice had a slight southern twang.

'Oh.' Only six o'clock? My sense of time was shot; I would have sworn it was past midnight. 'I thought it was later than that. It gets dark early now.'

'Are you . . . Peter Geller?' he asked hesitantly.

'Yes. You're here to see *me*?'

'Sir . . . David Hunt sent me.'

I had gone to college with Davy. We had been in the same fraternity — Alpha

Kappa. Since Davy came from old money, he got in because his family had always belonged to Alpha Kappa. I got in because I was smart: all the jocks and rich kids needed help to keep up their GPAs. Sometimes I had resented it, being used, but it got me into all the parties, and I still graduated at the top of our class.

My life had been a downward spiral after college. I had landed a plum job at an investment bank, but overwork and my always-racing mind led to a nervous breakdown. Six months later, a taxi ran me over and left me permanently crippled. I lost touch with everyone I'd ever known and began trying to drink myself to death, until Davy called me out of the blue to help him out when he was being blackmailed. That had been five months ago. We'd had dinner and drinks a dozen times since then, rekindling our old friendship. In fact, earlier this afternoon I had been wondering what to give Davy for Christmas. He already had everything money could buy.

'Are you some sort of social worker?' I asked warily.

'No, sir! I'm Bob Charles.' At my puzzled look, he added, 'Cree's brother.'

'Got any I.D.?'

'Uh . . . sure.' He dug around his coat's inside pocket. 'Driver's license? Passport?'

'Either.'

He handed me a military passport. Marine Corps issue, and the name under his picture read 'PFC Robert E. Charles.'

I nodded, my mental wheels starting to turn. Cree was the actress-slash-model Davy had been talking about marrying. Like Cher and Madonna, she only used one name.

'I guess you better come in,' I said.

'Thanks.' He scooped up his duffel bag and entered my apartment, looking around curiously. I didn't own much these days: a worn yellow sofa, a pair of white-and-yellow wingback chairs, a battered coffee table, and thanks to the miracle of Ikea, two tall wooden bookcases mostly devoted to bric-a-brac. No clocks, no calendar, no TV — nothing to remind me of the outside world. Nothing to stimulate my mind and set it racing again.

'How is Davy?' I asked.

'Good. He and Cree just left for Cancún.'

'Oh? I thought he had business in New York tomorrow.' At least, that's what he'd told me over the weekend.

Bob shrugged. 'Cree's doing a photo shoot for *Sports Illustrated* — filling in at the last minute — so they decided to turn it into a vacation. They're flying out tonight. Probably already in the air.'

He pulled off his coat, revealing an off-the-bargain-rack suit. I waved vaguely at the sofa.

'Sit down. Let me clean up. I wasn't expecting visitors. If you want a drink, help yourself — there's beer in the fridge.'

★   ★   ★

Twenty minutes later, I'd washed my face, run a razor over a three-day growth of beard, combed my hair, and put on nearly-clean slacks and a sweater. I almost felt human again, and I'd gotten rid of the worst of the whiskey smell.

Unfortunately, I had also begun to sober up, and with returning mental sharpness came all-too-familiar pains in both legs.

Alcohol blunted my senses better than drugs; that's why I drank as much and as often as possible. I only stopped when I had to.

Finally I limped back out to the family room. Bob leaped up when he saw me, running one hand quickly across his nearly-shaved head and pulling his suit jacket straight.

'Let me guess,' I said, really studying him for the first time. His too-short hair and well-developed muscles screamed military. 'You just got out of the service and decided to pay your sister a visit. She suggested Davy might be able to find you a job.'

He gaped. 'Did you talk to Cree?'

Slowly I settled into one of the wingback chairs, folded my hands across my belly, and stretched out both legs; they hurt less that way.

I said: 'Why else would an ex-Marine come to Philadelphia, if not to see your sister and her fiancé? You're dressed up — I assume for a job interview — though I'd lose the baseball cap next time. But the *real* question,' I said, warming to the

116

subject, 'is why Davy Hunt sent you here.'

Bob frowned, brow furrowing. 'He said he trusted your opinion. If you think I'm good enough, he'll take me on.'

'In what capacity?'

'Bodyguard.'

I raised my eyebrows slightly. 'Davy needs a bodyguard?'

'My sister thinks so.'

After their problem with blackmailers, I understood Cree's concern. Davy's net worth ran somewhere upwards of fifty million dollars — more than enough to make him a target for opportunists.

I opened my mouth, but before I could say anything, the doorbell rang again. From outside came faint childish giggles.

'You can start by taking care of those kids,' I said to Bob. 'Ask them not to bother me again.'

'Sir!' Like a panther, he sprang to the door and threw it open. Ten-year-old boys scattered, screaming, as he gave chase. I heard Bob shouting something about 'whooping hides' if they bothered me again, then several doors slammed shut.

When he returned, he was grinning. 'I

love kids,' he said. 'I don't think they'll bother you again, sir. At least, not for a few days.'

'Thanks.' Maybe bodyguards had their uses.

'Then you'll give me a try?'

I stared at him blankly. 'I don't follow you.'

'Sir, I'm supposed to be your bodyguard for the next few days. You can kick the tires. Try me out. Make sure I'm everything I ought to be to keep David safe.'

'I don't *need* a bodyguard. I don't *want* a bodyguard. I leave my apartment once or twice a month at most!'

'David knew you'd say that.' His brow furrowed. 'He told me to tell you — beg your pardon, sir — to shut up and pitch in.'

Just like Davy to be blunt with me. Maybe I *did* object too much. Maybe it *did* take a kick in the pants to get me moving. But did I really need a bodyguard?

It wasn't for me, though. It was for Davy. If he valued my opinion this much

. . . well, I needed to get him a Christmas present anyway. This would be it, as I would let him know the next time I saw him!

'Very well.' I motioned unhappily with one hand. I'd need rent money soon, anyway. 'You can start bodyguarding in the morning. It's time I ran some errands, anyway.'

Rent money meant a trip to Atlantic City and the casinos. Sometimes having a trick memory helped, like when I needed to know the number of face cards played from an eight-deck blackjack shoe.

'It'll be over sooner if I start tonight, sir.'

' 'Over sooner'?' I chuckled. 'Bob, you sound like you don't want to babysit a seedy drunken cripple!'

'Sir!' He looked alarmed. 'I never said that!'

'Then you *do* want to baby-sit a seedy drunken cripple?'

'That's a fool's argument, sir.' He shrugged with wry humor. 'You know I can't win. I just thought you'd want me out by Christmas day.'

'I don't care. Start when you want. End when you want. It's all the same.'

'Thank you, sir.'

'Do you have a place to sleep?'

'Uh . . . not yet. I was hoping to bunk here.'

It figured. Why did I suddenly feel like Oscar Madison from *The Odd Couple,* with an eager-beaver Felix about to move in?

'There's only one bed,' I said, 'and I'm usually passed out in it.'

'The sofa is fine — after sleeping in a Humvee for six months, pretty much anything will do. Just give me a blanket and I'll be out like a log.'

'There's one in the linen closet.' I jerked my head toward the back of the apartment. 'And an extra pillow on the top shelf.'

Using my walking stick, I levered myself unsteadily to my feet. My legs ached again. Slowly I limped toward my bedroom, thoughts of Jack Daniels and sweet oblivion dancing in my head.

★ ★ ★

Sometime later — it could have been hours, it could have been days — a loud humming filled my ears. It took a few minutes, but I finally realized the noise came from outside my skull. It shrilled on and on, incessant and very annoying.

When I couldn't stand it any longer, I rolled over and opened my eyes. Daylight leaked in around the blinds, casting a pallid gray light over my bedroom. Groaning, I got my feet to the floor and sat up.

The world swung and tilted. My head throbbed and my eyes burned. It had been a long while since I'd felt this sick. Usually when pain and nausea and headaches hit, I can lie still and wait for them to pass. This humming grated on my nerves so much, though, that I rose and stumbled toward the door.

When I entered the kitchen, the noise grew louder. But what brought me up short was the brilliant, blinding light.

Every surface gleamed. Steel and chrome and glass shone and glistened. The burnt-out bulbs in the ceiling fixture had been replaced, the dishes in the sink had been washed, and my months-old collection of pizza boxes had disappeared from the counter. Underfoot, the white-with-gold-specks linoleum had a new glossy sheen. Even the trashcan had a fresh white plastic liner.

The humming came from the family room. Bob Charles slowly moved into view, pulling a little canister vacuum around the floor, sucking up dirt and dust bunnies. He wore a clean white shirt and tie, but had on the same brown pants as yesterday.

'Good morning,' he called cheerfully, switching off the vacuum. 'Ready for breakfast?'

'What do you think you're doing?' I demanded. My voice came out as a croak.

'Tidying up.'

'Don't you know the difference between a maid and a bodyguard? I was still in bed!'

'It's ten-thirty in the morning. You've been asleep for more than sixteen hours, Pit. Half the day is gone!'

'Not asleep. Unconscious. Delightfully, *painlessly* unconscious. And how do you know my nickname?'

'Nickname?'

'Pit. Short for Pit-Bull. Got it in college.'

'Didn't you mention it yesterday?'

I shrugged. 'Maybe.'

But I hadn't. I could remember every word we had exchanged from the second I opened my front door to the second I'd gone to bed. Names, faces, facts, figures — I never forgot anything.

Maybe Davy had called me Pit, and Bob picked up on it subconsciously. I could only think of one other person besides Davy who still called me by my old nickname, and it seemed unlikely that Bob had ever met an organized crime figure like 'Mr. Smith,' as he called himself.

Bob was staring at my legs. I realized I hadn't put on a robe. Gray Jockey shorts didn't do much to hide the hideously scarred flesh running from my ankles to my hips.

Swallowing, Bob looked away. Pity — that was always the worst. It showed in his eyes.

'In case you're wondering,' I said bitterly, 'I got run over by a taxi.' Everyone always wanted to know what had happened, even if they were too embarrassed to ask.

'David didn't say anything about that.' Bob forced his gaze back to my face. 'He did tell me to take you out for breakfast today, though — on him.'

'I don't like going out. But maybe I'll make an exception this morning.' Time to pay Davy back for sticking me with Cree's brother. I used to read *Gourmet* magazine; I knew some *very* expensive places to eat in Philadelphia.

★   ★   ★

An hour later we left my apartment. Bob wanted to drive downtown in his battered old VW Rabbit, but I refused. Folding my legs into that tiny box of a car would have been torture.

Instead, we ambled up the sidewalk toward the Frankford El, our breaths pluming in the cold December air. The sun played hide-and-seek through holes in the clouds while an icy wind stirred leaves in the gutter. Far off, I heard an elevated train rumble past.

As we walked, Bob kept alert. Northwood is a small blue-collar section of Philadelphia, and it had definitely seen better years. But it was safe enough by daylight, and in the years I'd lived here, I had never had a problem beyond kids playing 'bait the cripple' with my doorbell.

'This neighborhood is a dump,' Bob said. 'You should find a better place to live.'

'I don't like change.'

'Those kids over there — ' He nodded toward a boarded-up row house across the street where three teenagers in stocking caps watched us with predatory eyes. 'They'd be happy to roll you for your cash.'

'I think they're about to try it,' I said. All three had gotten up and begun to cross the street toward us.

'Keep walking,' Bob said. He turned to face the three. 'I'll catch up in a minute.'

'Do you need help?'

'I can take care of a couple of kids.'

'Be careful.' My mind started racing, taking in every detail. 'The one on the left has a weapon in his pocket.'

'How do you know?' Bob demanded.

'He keeps touching it through his pants. I don't think the others are armed.'

'Get going.'

'But — '

'*Move!*'

Spoken like a true bodyguard. I wasn't about to argue.

Turning, I limped quickly up the street. Motion caught my eye as I reached the corner. I half turned as a dark-skinned man in a gray silk suit seized my arm and propelled me toward the street.

'Relax, Mr. Geller,' he said softly. 'Mr. Smith wants to see you.'

A white Lincoln Town Car roared up. Before it came to a stop, the back door popped open. My escort put his hand on the back of my head, pressing gently but firmly, and half guided, half pushed me into the lavender-scented back seat. Then he slid in next to me and slammed the door. We accelerated.

My abduction had taken less than five seconds. That had to be a record.

Twisting around, I gazed over my shoulder at the rapidly-receding figure of my bodyguard. Those three kids skirted my bodyguard and continued up the block. When Bob turned to check on me, a priceless look of shock appeared on his face. I had vanished. He began to run toward the Frankford El.

Turning back, I made myself comfortable, wincing a little as I un-crimped my legs.

'Hello, Pit,' said a smooth voice beside me.

'Mr. Smith.' I nodded to him. With his salt-and-pepper hair swept back and his neatly-manicured hands, he cut the perfect picture of a crime lord. As always, he wore an expensive Italian suit, blue this time with a white carnation at the lapel. 'If you wanted to talk to me,' I said, 'a simple invitation would have sufficed.'

'Not with your new, ah, *friend* looking on.' Smith smiled a predator's smile. Since our paths first crossed, he had developed quite an interest in me — due no doubt to my trick memory, which had dredged up his real name from a chance meeting many years before. Since then, I knew he had been researching my life — even going so far as bugging my phone.

'What brings you to my neighborhood?' I asked.

'I would like you to meet my associate, Mr. Jones.'

'Jones?' I raised my eyebrows and turned to the dark-skinned man next to me. 'You've got to be kidding.' Of African descent, with a diamond stud earring in his left ear, Mr. Jones seemed as fashionably well-groomed as Mr. Smith.

'Jones *is* my birth name,' said Mr. Jones gravely. 'Though I've been thinking of changing it to Tortelli to fit in better with the rest of the boys.'

Mr. Smith gave a snort, then added, 'Mr. Jones would not kid you about his name, Mr. Geller.'

'Of course not.' I sighed. Why did things like this always happen to me?

Then Smith lifted his left hand to my eye level. He held a miniature tape recorder. With his thumb, he pressed PLAY. Eleven beeps sounded — a phone being dialed. A moment later, I heard a woman answer:

'Hello?'

'Janice?' asked the voice of my body-guard.

'Yeah.'

'This is Bob. He went for it.'

She laughed. 'How fast can you get him to sign off on you?'

'A few days. God, he's depressing.'

'Put a bullet in his head when you're done. Put him out of his misery. Can't have him talking to Hunt, anyway.'

A chill went through me. Smith pressed the STOP button and returned the recorder to his pocket. It felt like I'd been struck in the stomach by a sledgehammer. Thank God I hadn't bothered to remove the bug in my telephone. Bob Charles had completely taken me in.

'Mr. Jones is in charge of your neighborhood,' Smith said. 'If you'd like your guest removed quietly, he will handle the extraction. As a personal favor to me, of course.'

'Removed?' I said. 'Extraction?'

'It is a specialty of mine.' Mr. Jones smiled, showing beautiful white teeth.

'Uh . . . that won't be necessary,' I said with a slight shudder. 'I'd prefer to handle him myself.'

Smith nodded. Mr. Jones passed me an ivory-colored business card with gold-embossed type. It said simply, JONES & ASSOCIATES and gave a phone number with a local exchange.

'If you need help, call me day or night,' Jones said. 'Any friend of Mr. Smith's is a friend of mine.'

'Thank you.' I pocketed his card. Not that I ever intended to call — but it would have been rude to refuse, and I thought it prudent to be very polite and very respectful to Mr. Jones.

Our Town Car glided to a stop in front of my apartment building. Mr. Jones got out, and awkwardly I did the same.

'Thank you,' I said to Mr. Smith. 'I owe you one.'

'Yes, you do,' he said.

Mr. Jones slipped back into the car, and they drove off together. I watched until they disappeared around the corner.

Suddenly, my life had gotten a lot more complicated.

★　★　★

Bob returned to my apartment half an hour later, looking cold and annoyed. I let him in and dead-bolted the door. Then I looked him over. Hard to believe he planned to kill me. I had always considered myself a pretty good judge of character, and he had fooled me completely. Damn it, I had actually begun to *like* him, with his goofy gungho act.

'No black eyes,' I said, 'and no bullet wounds, punctures, scuffs, or scrapes. Those boys must not have been much trouble after all.'

'They knew enough to steer clear of me.'

'See why I don't leave my apartment?' I limped back toward the kitchen. 'It's an unpleasant world. And it's much too tiring.'

'What happened to *you*?' Bob demanded, following. 'I couldn't find you anywhere!'

'Oh, a friend gave me a lift home. I

ordered a pizza. I hope you like pepperoni. It's the only topping that goes well with scotch.'

I sagged into a well-padded kitchen chair and took a slice from the takeout box. Sal's Pizza & Hoagies had dropped it off five minutes ago. I had already poured myself a large drink — mostly soda-water, with just a splash of booze to give it the right smell, mostly for Bob's benefit. I couldn't appear to change my alcoholic behavior lest it tip him off that I knew too much.

'Pepperoni is fine.' He got a beer from the fridge.

'Better stick with water,' I told him, wagging a finger. 'Bodyguards *never* drink on duty. Hazard of the trade.'

Silently he put it back. I could tell it annoyed him, though. One point for me.

★ ★ ★

After lunch, I announced my plans to visit the Free Library of Philadelphia . . . not our local branch, which specialized more in popular fiction than world-class research materials, but the large one on Vine Street in Center City. A plan had begun to form in the back of my mind . . . layers of deception, baited with promises of fast and easy money.

'The library? Can't you use the internet?' Bob asked. 'Everything's online now.'

'Not the material I'm looking for. And anyway, I'd still have to go to the library. I don't own a computer.'

I didn't add that I blamed computers in part for the information-overload that had led to my nervous breakdown.

* * *

On our second try, we reached the Frankford El without difficulty. I bought tokens; slowly we climbed up to the plat-form. Fortunately the train came quickly.

We sat in a nearly-empty car, and I focused my attention on the floor, analyz-ing stains and scuff-marks, trying not to look out the windows. Too much scenery, too much color and motion, tended to bring on anxiety attacks. I felt a rising sense of panic from Mr. Smith's warning. What would my fake-bodyguard do if I suddenly curled into a fetal ball on the floor?

'If we get separated,' Bob said suddenly, 'we need a plan. A place to regroup.'

I looked at his face. 'My apartment?'

'That will do if we're in this area. I meant someplace downtown, while we're out today.'

'There's a House of Coffee at 20th and Vine. That's half a block from the library.'

He nodded. 'Good.'

I went back to studying the floor. We rode in silence until we reached Race Street, and there we got out.

Shoppers bustled on the sidewalk, carrying bags and boxes, hurrying on holiday errands. Street vendors hawked caps and scarves and bric-a-brac. Brakes squealed and horns blared from the street. A bus rumbled past, spewing exhaust and carbon dioxide.

I felt a crawling sensation all over. Nervous jitters, just nervous jitters. Too many people and too much noise —

134

'Are you all right?' Bob asked.

I blinked rapidly, trying to stay focused. 'I feel overwhelmed — '

'Come on.' He grabbed my arm and propelled me forward. With his help, I managed to cross the street, and we headed toward Vine. I kept my gaze fixed on the sidewalk.

'Clear the way!' Bob bellowed. 'Sick man coming through!'

To my surprise, people actually moved for him — shoppers, businessmen, kids, even a pair of nuns — and we made rapid progress. Finally we passed through the double doors and into the sanctuary of the Free Library. A soothing silence washed over me. Better, better, so much better here. I closed my eyes, just breathing, and felt muscles starting to uncoil.

Bob said softly, 'If you need to go home — '

'I'll be fine. The outside world is . . . difficult sometimes. I shouldn't go into crowds on holidays.' I swallowed. 'I'm feeling better now. Really.'

The card catalog of my youth had been

replaced by computer terminals. I eased into a hard wooden chair, stretched my legs out as far as I could, and began my search for books on New York City banks.

Bob, with the occasional bored yawn, kept watch over my shoulder. I began jotting down titles and Dewey Decimal System numbers. When I had ten books selected, Bob took the list.

'I'll find them,' he said.

Within twenty minutes, he returned with eight of the ten volumes. Not a bad average — he made a fair research assistant.

The Manhattan Federal Trust sounded like a good choice. After suffering a series of financial losses in the late 1960s, it merged with Third Continental Loan, forming the Manhattan Third Federal Loan and Trust. It suffered a huge loss in 1973, when one of its armored cars had been hijacked. A half-dozen name-changes, mergers, and acquisitions later, I lost the trail in a 1991 Savings and Loan collapse. There didn't seem to be a surviving corporate entity.

I sat back. Yes, it would do nicely.

'Why do you care about this particular bank?' Bob asked suddenly.

'My father did some work there a long time ago,' I said. 'Can you find microfilm of back issues of the *New York Times?* I need to see July, 1973.'

'The whole month?'

'Yes. And maybe part of August.'

'You're the boss.' Shrugging, he went to find a librarian.

Meanwhile, I returned to the computerized card catalog and began looking up volumes on the U.S. legal system — choosing more for titles than content. I had no intention of reading them if I could avoid it.

'You're in luck,' Bob announced when he finally returned. 'They have the *New York Times* going back over a hundred years on microfiche. A lady is setting up the viewer now. They have a private room you can use, too.'

'Excellent!' I beamed as I handed over my new list. 'When I'm done, I'll need these books. Can you find them?'

'Sure.'

When he glanced at the titles, his eyes

widened. Volumes like *Circumventing the American Tax System, Overseas Tax Havens,* and *Criminal Statutes of Limitations: A State by State Guide* must have caught him by surprise.

'What are you planning?' he asked.

'Bodyguards aren't supposed to ask questions,' I said with a wink. 'I'm doing some research.'

'If this is illegal, I want to know. I might be held responsible as an accomplice — '

I laughed. 'Since when is research a criminal act? I'm thinking of writing a book.'

He frowned, clearly unsatisfied. But I offered no more explanations.

'Where do I go for the *Times*?' I asked.

'Over here.' Turning, he led the way to a small room at the back of the library. An elderly woman had a machine set up for me, and while Bob went off to find my legal books, I began to skim newspaper headlines. Minutes ticked by. My bodyguard returned with a stack of hardbacks, then settled into the chair next to mine.

Finally I found what I wanted: an article dated July 19, 1973. Five men made off with an estimated half million dollars in cash by hijacking an armored truck on the Brooklyn Bridge in broad daylight. It had been a daring robbery, ably executed.

'Way to go, Dad!' I muttered just loud enough for Bob to hear. Never mind that I hadn't been born yet when the robbery took place — thanks to my accident, I looked thirty years older than my actual age.

I printed out the article, folded it up, and stuck it in my shirt pocket. *Bait.* The library charged thirty cents for the printout, and I paid the lady happily.

'That's all I needed from the *Times*,' I said as I limped out of the room. I found an empty reading table and pretended to study tax evasion and statutes of limitations for the next half hour. The volumes seemed interminable.

At last, just when I couldn't take it any more, my stomach growled, announcing dinnertime. Another chance to gouge my assassin-bodyguard? I'd see how far I could run up his credit cards before letting him off the hook.

'I don't think Davy would mind springing for dinner instead of breakfast,' I told Bob, closing *Offshore Flight: Where and How to Take Your Money.*

'Probably not,' he said.

'There's a little seafood house around the corner called Charley's Red. Supposed to be pretty good, too.'

He perked up. 'I could go for some surf and turf.'

'You won't be disappointed.'

How could he be? It was a four-star restaurant with a wine list to die for.

★ ★ ★

Dinner was sublime. I ordered a bottle of Dom Perignon Rose 1988 with my caviar-and-truffle-stuffed lobster *à la* Charley. As I kept telling Bob throughout the meal, 'Don't worry, it's on Davy.'

Bob could only grin and nod. Finally, after a delightful chocolate soufflé followed by a glass of aged port, I could eat no more. I leaned back and patted my too-full belly.

Bob received the check and blanched.

Dinner for the two of us came to almost $750, I saw. Not including tip.

'They expect a 25% gratuity,' I told him, feeling generous: service *had* been exceptional.

'I . . . I'm afraid I can't, sir.' He gulped. 'There's only a couple hundred left on my credit card. David was going to reimburse me!'

'Oh.' So much for running up Bob's credit cards. The possibility that my bodyguard might be broke had never occurred to me. 'I'll handle it, then.'

I pulled out my AmEx. At least I knew Bob's finances now. Could I somehow use that to my advantage? I would have to think on it.

After I signed the credit card receipt, I found I could barely stand. So much for keeping my head clear. I had no choice but to agree to a taxi — which Bob said he would pay for, to make up for dinner. We rode in warmth and comfort back to my apartment.

There, I set my trap. I accidentally 'forgot' to remove the robbery article when I tossed my shirt into the bathroom hamper. I carefully left the lid up and the article in plain sight. Neat-freak that he was, I knew Bob would rush to close the hamper's lid, and when he did, he would spot the printout.

If he didn't conclude that my father had been in on the armored car heist, he was dumber than he looked. That, plus the research on offshore tax havens, painted me as a criminal at work . . . something he could try to turn to his advantage.

'Good night!' I said as I headed to my bedroom with a fresh bottle of whiskey. I carried it mostly for show; I had no intention of clouding my mind further tonight. 'Oh, I'll be up early — we have to go to Atlantic City tomorrow.'

'Want me to drive?' he offered.

'No need. Casinos return your bus fare in quarters when you get there, plus they sometimes throw in coupons for lunch and other freebies.' I had a drawer full of Golden Nugget tee-shirts to prove it.

★   ★   ★

As I lay in bed, thoughts racing, I mentally reviewed the recording Mr. Smith had played for me — and realized I had made a huge mistake.

Every button on a telephone keypad has a different sound. Since I remembered each tone on Mr. Smith's recording perfectly, it was a simple matter to match them up to numbers. Two seconds later, I had Janice's phone number. If I'd thought of it in time, I could have used a reverse directory at the library to look up her name and address.

Calling myself a drunken idiot, I picked up my phone's receiver, punched number 4 so the dial tone went away, and said in a low voice: 'Please tell Mr. Smith I'm going to the Azteca Casino on the nine o'clock bus tomorrow morning. When I get there, I'd like my bodyguard's complimentary drink spiked — something that will tie him up in the bathroom for an hour or so. I'm going to win a million dollars at the blackjack tables. Don't worry, I'll give it back. If Mr. Smith is willing to help, I'll owe him another favor. If not — well, I'll manage on my own.'

I hung up. Then I opened my night table's drawer and removed four pens from the neat row inside, along with an unused pocket notebook. In tiny, cribbed lettering, I began making lists of fictional transactions using several different colors of ink and alternating between sloppy and neat handwriting. First came dates, then names of various casinos, and amounts I had won. At the bottom of each page, I noted the anonymous Swiss or Brazilian bank account into which the money had been wired. My fictional net worth climbed rapidly into the millions.

Of course, I included all the secret pass codes anyone might need to get the money out. I emphasized that part on the inside front cover: *Funds not accessible without account numbers and pass codes.* Bob would read those words first when he opened the notebook.

★ ★ ★

My legs and back ached fiercely the next morning. When I couldn't take the pain any more, I rose and stumbled into the bathroom. I gulped four aspirins with a glass of tepid tap water. God, I needed a real drink.

Someone had lowered the hamper's lid. I peeked inside. The printout in my shirt pocket had been removed, then put back — but not quite folded properly. Sloppy, sloppy work.

Returning to my room, chuckling to myself, I dressed in black Dockers and a navy blue shirt — more leftovers from my Wall Street days — then took a small suitcase from my closet and began to pack . . . underwear, socks, shirts, pants. Everything I'd need for an extended trip. I needed to convince Bob I planned on fleeing the country.

My bodyguard appeared in the doorway. 'Going somewhere?'

'In case I decide to spend the night.'

He nodded. 'I'll bring my bag, too.'

*　*　*

An hour later we were on the bus. The drone of wheels on pavement, the murmur of little old ladies on their weekly gambling junket, the soft hiss of recycled air from the blowers overhead — I found it all curiously soothing. As I let myself relax, I began to open up and chat confidentially with Bob . . . part two of my plan.

'My father used to be involved with organized crime,' I confessed in a low voice. Never mind that he had been a plumber. 'He hijacked that armored car on the Brooklyn Bridge. The one I read about yesterday.'

'What happened?' Bob asked. 'Was he caught?'

'Not caught,' I said. 'Killed. His body turned up in the New Jersey wetlands near where Giants Stadium stands today. He had a bullet in his head, mob execution-style. I don't know what happened to the money, but I found out who did the hit a few years ago.'

'Who?'

'Well . . . let's just say he's come a long way in the last thirty years. He runs the Azteca Casino. That's why I gamble there a lot — every dollar I take away is a little piece of my revenge.'

He looked puzzled. 'I thought odds favored the house.'

'For most games.' I chuckled. 'You'd never guess I'm worth nearly as much as Davy Hunt, would you?'

He gaped at me. 'Then why are you stuck in that shabby little apartment? You should live like a king!'

I lowered my voice confidentially. 'Because,' I said, 'I don't want to attract the IRS's attention. If I started spending hundreds of thousands of dollars, they'd want to know where I got it.'

'The tax havens,' he said slowly. 'That's why you were researching them!'

'Bingo.'

He frowned. 'Why are you telling *me*?'

'Because,' I said grandly, 'this is it. Today is my final day. I'm going to make one last big score and retire to Brazil while I wait for the statute of limitations on income tax evasion to pass. I want you to come with me as my bodyguard and assistant. I'll need help, and I think you're the man for the job.'

He chewed his lip thoughtfully. This was a lot for him to consider. Would he go for it?

'If you're worried about salary,' I

added, 'I'll pay you a lot better than Davy — starting with a $20,000 signing bonus as soon as our plane lands. That buys a lot in South America. When we come back, we'll both be set for life. What do you say?'

'It's a deal!' He offered his hand, and we shook on it.

Bait taken — hook, line, and sinker.

★　★　★

Our bus rolled into Atlantic City on schedule and stopped at Bally's. We filed off with the old people, collecting vouchers for $20 in quarters, redeemable inside at the information booth. I shivered in the brisk wind while Bob collected our luggage. I should have worn a heavier coat.

'What next?' he asked, setting the bags down on the sideway.

'Go in and get our quarters, then we'll walk over to the Azteca.'

He then ran inside with our vouchers. A few minutes later he came back carrying two rolls of quarters. Then, carrying our bags, we ambled toward the Azteca.

Shaped like a South American pyramid, the hotel-casino offered three hundred and thirty luxury hotel rooms, most with views of the Boardwalk and the Atlantic Ocean. The entire ground floor consisted of slot machines, gaming tables, bars, restaurants, shops, and two theaters for concerts and stage shows.

I surveyed the elbow-to-elbow holiday crowds. Too loud, too bright, too busy . . . your typical Atlantic City gambling hall. From experience, I knew I would need several stiff drinks to make it through the day. Adrenaline would keep me going for now, though.

'Where do we start?' Bob asked.

'Check our coats and bags,' I said, 'then take the quarters and play the slots slowly. Pretend you don't know me, but watch my back. Things will get crazy when I start winning big.'

'How did you deal with it in the past?'

'I always kept my winnings under ten thousand per casino so they wouldn't catch on and blacklist me. Today, though,

I'm going for broke. A million or more, all from the Azteca.'

He whistled. 'You can do that?'

'Trick brain, remember?' I tapped my forehead with an index finger. 'Don't worry, I'll win. Just keep your eyes open and watch my back.'

Without another word, I limped to the line of blackjack tables. I kept going until I found one where a cute Asian lady was shuffling fresh decks, and I took the chair farthest to the left. I'd see everyone else's cards before mine. With 416 cards in play, knowing how many of each denomination remained in the shoe gave me a decided advantage, especially as we got toward the end.

I removed two hundred dollars from my billfold — gambling seed money, normally kept under my mattress — and bought a stack of chips. A man slid into the empty seat next to mine. I recognized Mr. Smith from the faint lavender scent.

'Good morning,' I said without looking in his direction.

'That was quite a boast you made,' he said. 'A million dollars at blackjack?'

'I can do it, as you know.'

He said, 'That's why I'm here. I have to protect the casino's interests. You are a very dangerous man, Mr. Geller.'

He set a tray of chips on the table before him — all bright pink and all stamped $100. He anted one. I risked $5. The three others at our table bet between $5 and $20.

The dealer began to draw cards from the shoe. A smattering of face cards and numbers for the others, a pair of jacks for Mr. Smith, a king and a four for me. Smith split his jacks, then hit for a twenty and a nineteen. I hit and drew an eight — busted. The house held at seventeen.

Nineteen cards gone. Four percent of the deck. A couple more hands and the odds would tilt in my favor.

Mr. Smith collected $200. The dealer swept away my $5 chip. We repeated. Mr. Smith won another $100, and I lost another $5. Repeat. I had a push, Smith lost. Repeat, and we both won.

A blonde in a skimpy mock-Aztec costume and too much eye-shadow approached. She had drinks on a tray.

'Compliments of the house,' she said, setting them in the blackjack table's built-in cup holders. Ginger ale for Mr. Smith, watery scotch-and-soda for me.

'Thanks.' I gulped mine in three swallows. 'Bring me two more,' I said before she disappeared.

Three more hands, sixty-seven cards burned. I increased my bet to $25. I split aces, then doubled down — easy wins. Three hands later, I increased my bets to $50. By that point, my initial investment had swelled to eight hundred dollars. Then twelve hundred. Then sixteen hundred.

Our dealer trashed the cards and began shuffling fresh decks together. My drinks arrived.

'You're good,' said Mr. Smith, nodding.

'Yes,' I agreed. I swallowed scotch-and-soda and felt myself relaxing, falling into the groove.

Suddenly Smith asked, 'Would you like to play at a high-stakes table with the house's money? Management uses shills to keep the action hopping. There's nothing like a big spender on a winning streak to stir up the crowd.'

'What about my bodyguard?'

'He's having that special drink you ordered right now.'

Casually, I glanced over at the slots. Bob was chatting with a different waitress in a mock-Aztec outfit. She held out a little plastic glass of what looked like cola, and he took it. As he sipped, he casually glanced in my direction, but showed no sign of recognizing me. Good boy.

'Ten minutes,' said Mr. Smith, 'and you'll be on your own.'

Ten minutes. Eight to ten hands.

'I can wait that long.'

* * *

It took almost fifteen minutes for Bob's drink to take effect. But when it hit, he hightailed it for the men's room at warp speed, leaving me alone.

I finished my hand — a $240 win — and tossed the dealer a $20 chip. Mr. Smith gathered up his winnings. By my count, I now had $7,600 in front of me.

'Follow me,' Smith said.

He threaded his way through the black-jack and craps and roulette tables to a small door marked PRIVATE: EMPLOY-EES ONLY. Inside, the noise and bustle of the casino gave way to fluorescent lights, cheap blue carpeting, and stark white walls broken only by glass doors showing tiny offices.

At the office marked CASINO MANAGER, Smith went in. I followed.

'Harvey,' he said to the pudgy-faced man at the desk, 'this is Mr. Geller, the guest I told you about.'

'Hiya, Mr. Geller.' Harvey wiped a sweaty hand on his pants before offering it to me. We shook. He went on, 'I have your paperwork ready.'

'Paperwork?' I asked.

'Legal forms you have to sign.'

'Lawyers run everything now,' said Mr. Smith half apologetically. 'In the old days, Harvey would have broken your legs if you tried to skip with the casino's money. Now he'll have you arrested.'

'What a kidder!' Harvey said, laughing. 'Can you imagine *me* breaking anyone's legs?'

Actually, I couldn't. But since Mr. Smith seemed serious, I gave a shrug and a smile.

Harvey held out a clipboard. I skimmed the one-page form — *I, Peter Geller, acknowledge that I am playing with the Azteca Casino Corporation's money, yada yada yada. I hereby warrant that all monies won or lost remain the sole and exclusive property of the Azteca Casino Corporation and will be surrendered before I leave the premises.*

Harmless enough. I signed, pressing hard for three carbon-less copies.

As soon as I finished, Harvey handed me the yellow copy from the bottom. Then he pushed a chip caddy loaded with gold chips stamped $1,000 across his desk. Ten stacks of ten chips each — one hundred thousand dollars. My hands began to tremble, and it wasn't from alcohol this time. I had never had this much money before . . . even if it wasn't mine to keep.

'What about my earlier winnings?' I asked.

'Give me your chips,' said Harvey.

I did so. Harvey counted them quickly, took a lockbox from his drawer, opened it, and peeled seven crisp thousand-dollar bills and six hundreds from a roll. Without comment, he passed them to me.

'Thanks.' I tucked them into my billfold.

'Come, Pit,' said Mr. Smith with a smile. 'A fortune awaits!'

★　★　★

My bodyguard still hadn't returned. Uneasy and suddenly self-conscious, I settled down in the well-padded leather highboy seat at the left side of a high-stakes table in the center of the casino. Velvet ropes cordoned the players off from the general public, and floodlights bathed our seats in a warm yellow glow. Overhead, a blue neon sign blinked HIGH STAKES PLAYERS ONLY — $100,000 MINIMUM. I was the only player.

A young guy with his blond hair in a crew cut nodded to me, then began unsealing fresh packs of cards. As he shuffled, an elderly man with a string tie and cowboy hat settled into the highboy next to me. A girl brought him a tray with a quarter million dollars in chips. A few seconds later, an Arab — complete with robes and bodyguards — took the seat farthest right. I noted how the casino staff called him 'your highness' and brought him drinks and bowls of green and red Christmas M&Ms without being asked. He had to be a regular.

I definitely felt out of my league.

Cowboy-hat seemed to sense my uneasiness. He jabbed me in the ribs with an elbow and said, 'First time here in the spotlight, huh, son?' He had a slight drawl. I noticed the heavy silver ring on his left index finger said A&M — probably Texas A&M University.

'Yes, sir,' I said.

'Internet money?' he asked.

'Mob money.'

Cowboy-hat got real quiet after that. I shifted uneasily in my chair. Then Smith returned and patted me on the shoulder.

'Good luck,' he said.

'Thanks. You're not playing?'

'I'll check back later. I have other duties.'
'Of course.'

Our dealer cleared his throat. 'Ready, gentlemen?'

I threw out a $1,000 chip. Time to get the ball rolling.

★　★　★

If only it had been my money. Never had I seen such a lucky streak.

I won my first six opening hands as I began to count cards. I won most of the middle hands where I knew enough to guess what might turn up. I won all the late hands, where the odds had shifted in my favor. Weird, wacky, wonderful luck — where were you when I needed you, when that taxi ran me down?

My winning streak continued throughout the first hour. Shoe after shoe, I beat the house consistently. The dealer began paying me in $10,000 chips. I hadn't even known that denomination existed. My money grew . . . half a million, then nearly a million. Mr. Smith would never doubt me again.

And Smith had been right about the buzz a big winner created. Behind the velvet rope, a crowd gathered to cheer me on. I started to sweat; the whispers and bursts of applause pushed my senses toward overload. Those three watery scotch-and-sodas helped, but not nearly enough.

Suddenly I noticed Bob Charles at the front of the gawkers. He looked pale and shaky. He must have recovered from his sudden 'stomach ailment.'

'Mr. Smith says you need a drink,' a voice said at my elbow. It was the same girl who had drugged Bob. She held out a tray. 'Compliments of the house, sir.'

'Thanks.' Since everything in front of me belonged to the casino, I had no worries about being drugged.

It was another scotch-and-soda; I gulped it down. Strong this time, the way I liked.

'Bring me another?' I asked.

'Of course, sir.' She vanished.

Tex leaned in close and said, 'Better watch that stuff, if you expect to keep winning. Gotta stay sharp, son!'

'Drink or die,' I said unhappily. 'I can't function sober.'

He laughed. 'Then maybe I should take up drinking, the way my luck's running!'

His stack of chips had been cut in half over the last two hours. Further down the table, the prince barely held his own.

I bet $50,000 — and got a blackjack. Cowboy-hat drew to a 12 and busted. Too many face-cards still in play . . . with the dealer showing a five, I would have stayed.

My new drink came, and I downed it fast. The rising tide of voices began to grow muted; my hands stopped shaking. My world narrowed down to the cards.

But first, I reminded myself, I had to take care of Bob.

'I have to take a bathroom break,' I said to the dealer. 'May I leave my chips here?'

'Of course, sir.'

'Don't worry, son,' said Cowboy-hat. 'I'll keep an eye on 'em for ya!'

'Thanks.' I smiled wanly at him.

I rose, leaning heavily on my walking stick, and gave Bob a glance and a subtle follow-me jerk of my head. Then I limped to the men's room.

It was moderately busy inside. We stood

side by side at the urinals, waiting until we were alone. Then I handed him my billfold with the $7,600 still inside.

'I have my million,' I said. 'There's a travel agency across the street. Buy two one-way tickets to Rio de Janeiro. I doubt if there's a direct flight from Atlantic City, but we should be able to make it with a couple of connections. Cut it as close as possible. When it's time to go, signal me. I'll cash out and we'll run for the plane. As fast as a cripple like me can run, anyway.'

'Got it,' he said.

*　*　*

I returned to the high-stakes table and found Mr. Smith had replaced Cowboy-hat. My chips had not been touched. Fortunately for me, most of the watchers had dispersed.

Our dealer began shuffling new decks of cards.

'Is everything going as planned?' Smith asked.

'I think so.'

'I saw your friend leave. You should have let Mr. Jones remove him for you, you know.'

'Human life has value,' I said.

'You should watch out for yourself, not someone who's trying to kill you.'

I shrugged. 'Perhaps I made a mistake. But I like him, and I think he's basically a decent guy. He just took a wrong step somewhere.'

'Are you sure you won't change your mind?'

'I'm more stubborn than sensible. Besides, it's almost Christmas. 'Tis the season of brotherly love, and all that mushy holiday stuff. I couldn't have his 'removal' on my conscience.'

'What's next?' Smith asked.

'Bob is out buying tickets to Rio de Janeiro. He'll be on the afternoon plane. That's where you come in.'

'I suppose he needs a lift to the airport?'

'I'm going to cash out when he returns. I'll give instructions at the cashier's booth for the winnings to be wired into a non-existent Brazilian bank account. Then, on

162

my way out the door, someone can grab me, force me into a car, and drive off with me. Bob will think I'm being kidnapped and take off for Brazil alone.'

'Why would he?'

'Because,' I said smugly, 'he's going to have my little black notebook with all the pass codes and bank account numbers. He'll think he's struck it rich.'

'Until he gets there and finds out there's no money.'

'Right.'

'Then he'll come back, hunt you down, and kill you for making a fool out of him.'

'He'll stay there. I'm sure he'll call once he gets to Rio and finds out he's been duped. I'll simply tell him he'll be arrested for conspiracy to commit murder if he returns to the United States. I imagine you still have that recording.'

'Of course.'

'I'll borrow it and play it back for him. He won't dare return. End of problem!'

Smith shook his head. 'You overly complicate things, Pit. Remove him and move on with your life.'

'That's not an option.'

'Your plan is ridiculous.'

'But you'll help me,' I said.

He shrugged. 'I find it fairly amusing. But once it's done, I have a real job for you in Las Vegas. One for which you are uniquely qualified.'

'As long as I don't have to break the law,' I said, 'I'll go. I always keep my word.'

The dealer asked, 'Ready, gentlemen?' He had finished stacking the cards in the shoe.

Smith excused himself. The prince and I both anted, and our game began anew.

★　★　★

By the time Bob returned, I had won another hundred and forty thousand. A new crowd gathered beyond the velvet ropes. Bob eased his way to the front and signaled me by tapping his wristwatch. Time to catch our plane.

'That's it for me,' I said, rising. I tossed the dealer a $1,000 chip. 'Thanks for everything.'

'Thank *you*, sir!' he said, beaming.

I gathered my winnings onto a tray, then limped to the cashier's station. Mr. Smith sat comfortably ensconced behind the brass grill.

'How much did you win?' he asked in a low voice as I passed him my chips.

'One-point-two million,' I whispered smugly, 'plus change.'

'It's a good thing you were playing with the house's money. How soon do you want to be abducted?'

'As we leave. We'll go through the doors onto Atlantic Avenue. Do you have a pen and paper?'

'Here.' He slid them over to me.

I jotted down wiring instructions for the money and passed it back.

'Might as well go through the motions,' I said. 'May I have a receipt for the wire?'

Chuckling, he made one up. I tucked it into my little notebook, which I kept in hand as I limped off for the Atlantic Avenue doors. There Bob Charles waited impatiently, pretending to study a marquee. I paused beside him. From the corner of my eyes, I saw men in black suits starting to converge on us.

'I already wired the money to my Brazilian account from the courtesy counter. But I don't think they're going to let me leave here safely.' Casually I dropped the notebook. 'Cover that with your foot. Pick it up when I'm out the door — they can't find it on me. It has the pass codes for my anonymous bank accounts. If I can, I'll catch up at the airport.'

Without bothering to retrieve my coat or bag from the checkroom, I headed for the door. The bellman opened it for me, and shivering at the sudden cold, I stepped outside.

Smith's men followed on my heels — goons built like refrigerators. I had seen both of them before at Smith's illegal casino outside of Philadelphia.

A white Town Car sat idling in front, and they grabbed my elbows and hustled me inside. I didn't struggle.

As I twisted around, we accelerated into traffic. I glimpsed Bob running out the front door. He stood there, staring after me, a look of anger on his face.

He cared what happened to me. I saw

it, and in that moment I knew I had made the right decision. Better to handle him myself than let Smith and Jones do it. He *was* basically a decent guy.

'Thanks, fellows,' I said to the goons.

Mr. Smith sat in the front passenger seat. He opened a small window in the bulletproof partition separating our seats.

'Where next?' he asked. 'The airport?'

'Take a ten minute drive, then back to the casino. I have to pick up my coat and bag. Then I'll catch the bus home.'

'You heard the man,' Smith said to our chauffeur.

'Yes, sir!' he said.

The goons and I settled back.

* * *

We didn't even make it five blocks — police cars with blinking lights cut us off, front and back. Our driver slammed on the brakes; we fishtailed, then came to a screeching halt.

As uniformed officers leaped from their cars with drawn weapons, Smith's goons reached for their guns.

'Don't do that,' I said in a low voice. 'This has to be a mistake.'

A bullhorn blared: 'Get out of the car with your hands up!'

'I'm not happy, Pit,' said Mr. Smith. He got out of the car and raised his hands. The chauffeur and goons did the same.

Slowly, painfully, I followed.

'You are in big trouble,' Smith told the policemen who advanced. 'Do you know who I am?'

None replied. They forced his hands onto the roof of his Town Car and began frisking him. Another officer began reading us all our Miranda rights.

That's when I spotted Bob Charles sitting in one of the patrol cars. He must have gone running to the cops instead of taking off for Brazil with my money. I nodded to him, and he grinned back.

'That's him — that's Peter Geller!' he said, climbing out and pointing at me. 'They were kidnapping him!'

A police lieutenant took my elbow and drew me to one side. 'Mr. Charles flagged down a patrol car,' he said, 'and reported your abduction. He said you won big at the casino and they weren't going to let you keep it. Is that true?'

'No,' I said emphatically. I gestured at the Town Car and Mr. Smith. 'This is some kind of misunderstanding. I work for the casino. These men are all friends of mine. We were taking an early supper.'

The lieutenant frowned. 'What about the money he said you won? More than a million dollars, wasn't it?'

'Nonsense. I was playing with the casino's money. Here — see for yourself!'

I pulled out the yellow copy of the form I'd signed. The lieutenant scanned it, snorted, then said to the other cops:

'Let them go. We've made a mistake.'

'Thank you,' said Mr. Smith. He straightened his tie and jacket.

The lieutenant stalked back to Bob, and they exchanged heated words. Bob read the yellow form, then stared at me in disbelief. When the lieutenant made Bob get out and lean up against the hood of the police car, I watched with amusement.

Of course, the officer turned up two wallets — one of them mine — plus the notebook of bank account numbers and plane tickets. He studied them, then stalked back to me.

'Is this yours?' He held out my wallet.

'Yes. Bob was holding onto it for me.'

He frowned. 'And two tickets to Rio?'

'Also mine.'

'Notebook?'

'Yep. Mine.'

His eyes narrowed. He knew something odd had gone down, but for the life of him he couldn't figure it out.

'I think you all had better come with me to the station,' he said.

I shrugged. 'As you wish.' To Mr. Smith, I said, 'Perhaps you can recommend a good lawyer?'

'He'll meet us there,' Smith said grumpily, reaching for his cell phone.

★ ★ ★

I rode in the back of the police car with Bob. The cops hadn't bothered to handcuff either one of us. Mr. Smith and his goons were following in their Town Car.

'Are you insane?' Bob demanded. 'I just

saved your life! Why are you doing this to me?'

'Maybe I'm a little bit cranky, but I'm hardly insane.' I chuckled. 'You asked me to kick your tires, Bob. Congrats. You passed the test.'

His breath caught in his throat. 'A . . . test. This whole thing . . . '

'That's right. And I can *almost* recommend you to Davy Hunt.'

'Almost?'

'There's one matter you still have to take care of.'

He looked puzzled. 'I don't understand . . . '

'Janice.'

He paled. 'How — how do you know — '

'Trick brain, remember?' I grinned. 'Tell the police how Janice tried to set up Davy using the two of us, and I'll get you cleared of all charges by morning.'

★　★　★

Once Bob started talking to the police, he had quite a story to tell. When he got out of the Marines, an old girlfriend contacted him, got him to come to

Philadelphia, and told him she worked as the private secretary for a billionaire sleazebag named David Chatham Hunt.

A year ago, Janice had a romantic fling with her boss. Presents were given, promises were made . . . apparently, she expected the relationship to go farther than Davy did. When he broke things off and started dating a supermodel named Cree, she took it very hard.

Janice planned her revenge with meticulous care. As his private secretary, she knew Davy's position on the Board of Directors at Hunt Industries was provisional. Any hint of a scandal, and he'd get the boot. Davy couldn't allow that to happen.

And that's where Bob came in. Janice knew about my friendship with Davy, and she thought my personal recommendation would get Bob hired as bodyguard, cutting through a lot of red tape. Apparently she believed she could lure Davy into a final romantic tryst . . . one where Bob would be present to take blackmail photos.

It could have worked. Davy might well have fallen into her trap. I could easily envision my old friend having one last fling with his secretary, just to get her off his back.

Once Janice was arrested, she collapsed into hysterics at the police station, confessed everything, and ultimately pleaded guilty to conspiracy charges. Her case would never go to trial, saving Davy a lot of embarrassment.

Thanks to Mr. Smith's lawyer, Bob Charles ended up with probation and stern warnings from a judge. He never spent a single night in jail. Best of all, on my recommendation, Davy hired him as his personal bodyguard. I thought they would go well together. Bob had certainly proved himself to my satisfaction.

* * *

'And that's the whole story,' I said to Davy and Cree over Christmas dinner. Cree had cooked it herself — a beautiful roast goose with cranberry sauce, mashed sweet potatoes, green bean casserole, and a delightful selection of home-baked pies.

'Incredible,' Davy said, shaking his

head. 'You know what the worst part of this whole mess is?'

'What?' I asked.

'Janice was the best secretary I ever had.'

Cree punched him on the arm — hard.

'But my new secretary seems just as good,' he added quickly.

'Better,' said Cree. She turned to me. 'I picked him out myself. No more office romances, right, Davy?'

'Right!' he agreed. But he seemed a little wistful.

I chuckled. 'It took a long time and cost a small fortune, but what do you think of my present?' I asked.

'Present?' Davy scratched his head and looked at Cree, who shrugged. 'Did I miss something?'

I raised my wineglass in salute. 'For the man who has everything — a new secretary and a new bodyguard. Merry Christmas, Davy!'

4

Dog Pit

When the phone rang, I rolled over in bed and sighed. I knew who it was; no one but telemarketers and my old college friend David Chatham Hunt wanted to talk to me these days. And telemarketers seldom called this early on a Saturday morning.

Actually, I had been half expecting to hear from Davy. Tonight was his engagement party, and he wanted me there — enough to be a nag about it. This would be his third reminder of the week. Probably checking up to make sure I wasn't drinking myself into an early stupor. He didn't understand my use of alcohol was strictly for medicinal purposes; I could stop any time I wanted to. Since it blunted my pain better than morphine or codeine, I didn't often want to stop. But I had, today, for him. That's how much our friendship meant to me.

On the fifth ring, I picked up the receiver.

'You have reached the Geller residence,' I said in a mock British accent. 'Please leave your name and number after the bleep and someone will return your call when sober.' I pressed the '5' button for half a second.

'Very funny, Pit,' Davy said. 'You don't have an answering machine.'

'I hear they make great presents. My birthday is coming up. Hint, hint.'

'If you had one, you'd never answer the phone.'

'True.' He knew me too well.

'You realize,' Davy went on, 'this is the first time I've called and found you completely sober since college.'

'You can tell?'

'Your words aren't slurred. You must be lying down.'

I blinked. 'How does that follow?'

'You get a bit, ah, *testy* when you're in pain. You keep saying your legs don't hurt as much when you're not using them. You're in a good mood — humorous, joking — *ipso facto*, you're lying down.'

'You win a prize, Sherlock.' I laughed. 'I know why you're calling, Davy. Don't worry, I'll show up tonight. And I won't do anything to embarrass you or Cree.'

'That's not why I'm calling.'

I sat up, suddenly concerned, and an unexpected jolt of pain shot through my ruined legs. They were a byproduct of a run-in with a New York City taxi several years before. I sucked in a startled breath and tried to ignore it.

'What's wrong?' I demanded. 'You and Cree haven't broken up or anything — '

'Of course not!' He gave a derisive snort. 'I booked a limo to pick you up, and I wanted to let you know. Can you be ready at five o'clock?'

'Sure.' Very thoughtful of him. Davy, with a net worth well into the millions, could certainly afford a limousine. Normally I would have turned it down, but I knew tonight meant a lot to him. I'd be there in time.

'Five o'clock?' I frowned. 'The party doesn't start till eight.'

'Family dinner first — my parents and us. Besides, you know how Cree feels

177

about your beer-and-pizza diet.'

'Is she offering a home-cooked dinner?'

'She's at the market buying ingredients now.'

I grinned. Cree was an excellent cook, as Davy's slowly expanding waistline testified.

'I'll be there!'

★   ★   ★

The ride to Davy's place took half an hour. Ostentatious as always, he had sent a thirty-foot-long stretch limo to pick me up. The driver kept the partition between us closed and his comments to himself. I got that reaction sometimes. There are a lot of stupid people in the world who won't talk to cripples.

I killed time by sipping ginger ale (the limo's bar had been stocked with every soda imaginable but nothing even remotely alcoholic — Davy at work again), downing Motrin caplets to deal with the pain, and watching Action News on the tiny ceiling-mounted television. The usual parade of crimes, missteps, and indignities streamed past: rape, murder, celebrity divorce, burglary, even a gang fight in Kensington . . . half a mile from my apartment.

Then came a story that piqued my interest. The Society Bandit (as the press had dubbed him) had struck again. He worked parties in the wealthiest parts of Philadelphia and its Pennsylvania suburbs, making off with small but valuable items. Last night he had stolen an eight-inch bronze Rodin sculpture from the home of Dr. and Mrs. Ogden Marsala while they hosted a dinner benefiting Ethiopian relief efforts. They discovered the theft the following morning.

I had to laugh. There couldn't possibly be much of a market for hot Rodin sculptures. It was probably sitting on the thief's desk as a paperweight.

Then we turned off the road, passed through high wrought-iron gates (conveniently propped open for the party) onto a red paving block driveway, and circled a mermaid-encrusted marble fountain in front of the house. That three-story Victorian monstrosity Davy called home — all ten bedrooms and rambling seven thousand square feet of it — sat directly ahead. A kid with a flag waved us away from the miniature orange cones in front, so my driver edged onto the side lawn next to half a dozen white vans from Di Pesci Event Catering.

A small army of men and women dressed all in white, from chef's hats to sneakers, were unloading the vans. They carried items around the house toward what had to be a circus-sized red-and-white canopy, though I could only see one end of it poking around the house's east wing. I should have realized the party would be outside; there must be hundreds of people on Davy and Cree's guest list.

The chauffeur came around and opened the door for me, and I eased my way out, leaning heavily on my cane. Though my legs ached faintly, I had gotten off easy this trip. They would have been on fire had I taken the bus, as originally planned.

'Thanks,' I said.

He nodded. Still not a word. Maybe he was mute.

Slowly I limped around the line of vans

toward the house. When I rounded the last one, I drew up short. A giant of a man, burly and black-bearded, dressed in white like the rest of the caterers and carrying a large aluminum tray, blocked my path.

'Excuse me,' I said.

'No samples! No handouts!' he barked in a heavily accented voice. Russian?

Bristling, I drew myself up to my full height. He still towered over me.

'And you are . . . ?' I began.

'No time! Work now! You leave!'

He pushed around me, almost knocking me off my feet, striding briskly toward the canopy. I glared at his back. Crazy, absolutely crazy. I'd talk to Davy about him later. Time to find a new caterer.

Leaning on my cane, I limped slowly to the house. Then, as I climbed toward the front door, a four-legged tornado burst from the open doorway, snarling and barking and generally raising the alarm. He had the ears of a German shepherd, with maybe a hint of Doberman mixed in. And he had more teeth than any dog I'd ever seen before. Half my arm would have fit into that cavernous mouth with room to spare.

'Uh . . . nice doggie?' I said. Slowly I raised my cane. It didn't have a sword inside, but the silver handle would make a pretty good club if necessary.

'Angel! Heel!' called an unfamiliar voice from inside.

The dog sat instantly. But he kept his teeth bared, and low-decibel growls continued deep in his throat.

A second later a kid of perhaps eighteen or twenty trotted out. He wore his copper-colored hair in a buzz-cut, and he had a broad freckled face with ears that stuck out too much. Ripped jeans and a Green Day tee-shirt that had seen better days completed the picture. A relative of Davy's? He didn't seem dressed for the party. Though I supposed he still had several hours to change.

When his blue eyes swept over me without recognition, he frowned.

'Who are you?' he asked bluntly.

'Call off your dog. I'm an old friend of David Hunt's.'

'Can you prove it?'

'I forgot my friend-of-groom card.' I let a note of annoyance creep into my voice. 'So no.'

As if on cue, Davy himself appeared. I saw laughter in his cool blue eyes, though he kept his expression serious.

'Well, Pit?' Davy said. 'What do you think of Angel? Just got him!'

I regarded the beast warily. 'Then he's yours?'

'Yep!'

'Didn't you learn your lesson about not buying strange animals when your million-dollar racehorse died?'

'Nonsense. Angel isn't an animal, he's a home security system!'

I rolled my eyes. Dogs should be members of the family. Happy, trusted, tail-wagging members. A boy's best friend . . .

'Mr. Hunt?' said the buzz-cut kid. 'Should I introduce him to Angel?'

'Sure.'

The kid said, 'Angel! Friend!'

Still growling, Angel crept close to me on his belly and raised his head. He had a musky, very doggy odor.

'Let him smell your hand,' the kid said.

'Will I get it back?' I asked. The growling unnerved me.

'Angel is well trained.'

'That doesn't answer my question!'

Davy said, 'Stop being a baby and let my dog smell your hand, already!'

Cautiously I did so. Sure enough, Angel gave a few sniffs, then lost interest. Even his growls died away. Apparently I would be tolerated now.

'Angel! Come!' said the kid. The dog obeyed and got a treat for his efforts. The pair trotted back inside.

'Was that monster your idea?' I asked.

'Well . . . not really. Cree's been worried about the Society Bandit. Mom suggested a dog. Oscar trained hers.'

I rolled my eyes. 'When someone gets bitten and you get sued, you'll be sorry.'

He chuckled. 'Always the pessimist, Pit. Come on in, Cree's in the kitchen.'

★　★　★

A dozen white-shirted workers packed the kitchen, taking up every available inch of counter-space. They were fussing over aluminum trays packed with hors d'oeuvres, Swedish meatballs, colorful pasta dishes, slabs of raw salmon and filet mignon, vegetables, and more . . . it seemed Davy and Cree had spared no expense on the food.

Only the center island remained relatively clear. Cree and Davy's mother were both there, surrounded by spices, mixing bowls, and ingredients. Davy's mother was smoking — and I noticed how Cree stood carefully upwind.

'Peter!' Cree cried when she saw me, voice musical with that rich Louisiana accent. 'How are you!'

Her light brown skin made a startling contrast to the dazzling white of her teeth and the liquid green of her eyes. You could see why she had such a successful modeling career. A striking face, a striking figure. Smart to boot.

I grinned. 'I'm good. You look fabulous, Cree!'

'Thank you, my friend!' Laughing, she held up her right hand. 'What do you think?' she asked.

I focused on the engagement ring. The

huge diamond sparkled quite amazingly. It must have cost a fortune. I whistled.

'Wow!' I said. 'It's huge!'

'The one I wanted her to have was nicer,' said Davy's mother from behind Cree. Tall, ash-blonde, and aging well thanks to at least two facelifts, Mrs. Hunt looked only a few years older than Cree . . . if you ignored the smoker's pallor and an unnatural tightness to the skin around her eyes and neck. 'It belonged to my mother, and to my grandmother before her — a beautiful white diamond surrounded by sapphires . . . '

Cree rolled her eyes, but not so Constance Hunt could see. Clearly this was an old argument.

'And how are you, Mrs. Hunt?' I said, forcing a smile. Best to change the subject.

'Don't I know you?' she asked, puffing on her cigarette and studying my face. 'You look familiar, but I can't quite place you . . . '

'Yes, ma'am,' I said. 'We met at Davy's college graduation. I'm Peter Geller. Davy and I were in the same fraternity. I must say you look as beautiful as ever.'

'Why, thank you!' She positively beamed. Then her gaze drifted down to my cane and her frown deepened. 'You gave the valedictorian speech that year, didn't you?'

I nodded. 'You have an excellent memory.'

'Pit graduated at the top of our class,' Davy said, putting a hand on my shoulder proudly. 'Smartest guy I know. He remembers everything he's ever seen or read.'

'Trick brain.' I shrugged. 'But enough about me,' I said. 'This is supposed to be your day, Cree.' I took her hand and looked at her ring more closely. 'It really suits you. Is that a platinum setting? This stone must be fifteen carats!'

'Fifteen and a half,' Davy said smugly.

'Congrats!' I said to them both, and I meant it.

Whatever she had been working on with Mrs. Hunt smelled pretty good. Cooking was Cree's hobby; though she hardly ate herself, she enjoyed over-stuffing everyone around her. Eating by proxy, I guess. Bowls of chopped, minced, and crushed ingredients surrounded the six-burner gas stove. Onion, garlic, carrots . . . and plenty of green leafy things I couldn't identify. I thought I smelled fresh spearmint, though. I sniffed appreciatively.

I asked, 'What are you cooking?'

'Vegetarian Creole meatballs,' she said, 'made with black rice.'

'Black?' I raised my eyebrows doubtfully. 'Vegetarian?'

Mrs. Hunt snorted. 'That was my reaction, too, Peter. Meatballs should have *meat*. Otherwise they're some sort of weird dumpling.'

'Trust me,' Cree said. 'Low calorie and delicious.'

'If you say so . . . ' I still had my reservations. Rice should not be black, even Cajun style.

'This is going to be quite a party,' I said to no one in particular, staring at the bustle of visiting cooks. Everything seemed chaotic, but each worker had to know his or her job. Even the Mad Russian was there now. I caught him staring at me, but he quickly averted his gaze when he saw I had noticed. Some people reacted that way to cripples, too.

Guilty conscience, no doubt.

'Of course,' Mrs. Hunt said, 'this is going to be *the* social event of the season. Paolo Di Pesci has *never* disappointed me.'

'He's the caterer,' Davy explained.

'I know,' I said. 'His name is plastered all over the vans outside.'

A voice called from the next room: 'Connie! Are you bothering the kids again?'

'No!' said Mrs. Hunt.

Cree called, 'It is never a bother, Mr. Hunt!'

Davy's father appeared in the doorway to the dining room, a ruddy-faced man in his late fifties slowly going to fat. He wore an olive-colored Italian suit several years out of style, but it didn't quite fit properly. He must have put on sixty or seventy pounds since Davy's and my graduation. What was his first name? A second later my memory dredged it up: Robert. Robert Chatham Hunt. ('Call me Moose,' he had said to me at Davy's graduation party, a bit drunk from the vodka martinis that he had been mixing.

'You're a fellow Alpha' — referring to our fraternity — 'so there's no standing on formality.' *Moose Hunt*. There must have been quite a story behind it, though I hadn't had the nerve to ask.)

'Come on, Connie,' Mr. Hunt said with a wink. 'Let the kids have their fun. I've got martinis waiting in the library . . . ' His gaze settled on me. 'You're Pit, right? David said you would be here. Pleased to meet you, son.'

'Likewise, sir.' Clearly he didn't remember me. 'Call me Peter, please.'

'Sure.'

'Did you say you'd mixed martinis?' My legs were starting to ache from too much use; Motrin just didn't work that well anymore. And my hands had begun to tremble slightly. I could use a drink to steady myself.

'Go on, all of you!' Cree said, though I suspected it was more to get rid of her mother-in-law-to-be than the rest of us. 'Too many cooks . . . '

'Goodbye for now,' Davy said. Instead of a peck on the cheek, he gave her a passionate kiss . . . that went on and on.

190

Davy's mother broke it up by clearing her throat disapprovingly. Giggling like school kids, Davy and Cree held hands instead. Sickening, all of it.

'Come on, come on,' Davy's father said. 'You can't let martinis sit forever.'

'Right!' I started toward him.

Mrs. Hunt said, 'If you want, Cree, I can have Paulo give you a hand. His people can finish up your dumplings while we relax and enjoy ourselves. That's what caterers are *for*, my dear.'

'Really, I prefer to do it myself.' Cree slipped off her engagement ring and set it behind the stove, then began kneading ingredients together as if they were Mrs. Hunt's neck. Tofu, herbs, then onion and garlic, then minced carrots. She began pulling chunks from the slightly gooey mass and rolling them into balls, which she dropped onto a baking sheet in neat rows. I hated to admit it, but they *did* smell pretty good.

Suddenly frantic barking sounded outside. Davy's alarm-dog had gone off.

'Sounds like Angel found another guest,' I said with a laugh.

Cree frowned. 'Davy, you need to lock that creature up. He is going to ruin the party!'

'With the Society Bandit around?' Mrs. Hunt said. 'Let him do his job!'

Davy said reassuringly, 'He'll calm down when he gets used to our routine.'

'A dog like that won't stop a real thief,' I said. 'You're just going to terrify poor innocent guests. Me, for instance!'

'You're hardly innocent,' Davy said.

'How about those martinis?' Mr. Hunt said. 'Properly stirred, never shaken!'

Cree pointed a tofu-and-herb encrusted finger in my direction. 'You are exactly right, my friend!' she said to me, accent musical. 'David, listen to Peter for once!'

'You're both dog-haters,' Davy said. 'I'll go see what's up with Angel.' He started for the back door.

'And tell that kid to be more polite to potential guests!' I called after him. 'Crippled old men don't pose much of a threat to the household silver!'

'Thirty-one isn't old!' Davy said. 'We're the same age, Pit! Remember?'

'Hah!' I said. I turned to Mr. Hunt.

'That drink sounds pretty good to me. What kind of vodka did you use?'

'Russian, of course — '

Davy paused in the doorway. 'Pit, you might want to hold off till after dinner — '

Then the buzz-cut kid burst in, out of breath, face pale. Angel was nowhere in sight, but the frantic barking continued.

Suddenly I had a premonition of disaster. The head chef mauled over a dropped fillet mignon? Davy's grandmother treed?

'There's a fire!' the kid cried. 'Call 9-1-1!'

A startled hush fell over everyone in the room.

'What!' Davy gaped at him. 'Where?'

'Out back!'

That had to be why Angel was barking his head off. Maybe he wasn't such a menace after all.

The barking grew even more frantic, if that was possible. Cree grabbed a towel and began wiping her hands clean.

'Oh dear, oh dear!' cried Mrs. Hunt. 'Robert? Do something!'

'Show me where it is!' Davy said to the kid.

'Out here!' he said. He turned and ran. Davy followed, with his parents close on his heels.

To Cree, I said, 'I'll call the fire department.' I hurried to the wall phone. Davy had a portable handset; I grabbed it and dialed quickly.

'Thank you,' Cree said. She hurried after the Hunt clan.

All the cooks gave chase, too. Nobody wanted to miss out on the excitement, it seemed.

'We have a fire,' I told the emergency services woman. I gave her Davy's name and address, my name, and all the other details they wanted.

Holding the portable handset, I went in the direction of the hysterical barking, leaning on my cane and keeping the phone receiver to my ear. Yes, I would stay on the line until the police arrived. No, I wasn't in any immediate danger. At least, not as far as I knew.

I reached the back porch. The fire was not at the caterer's tent, where I had expected it, but at the freestanding garage where Davy housed his car collection. Black smoke billowed out. And Angel stood there barking nonstop.

Luckily two of the cars were parked by the house — the silver BMW convertible I liked so much and the red Porsche Cree drove. That left the Bentley, the Lamborghini, and two Cadillacs still inside.

I joined Davy, who was pacing and cursing nonstop in front of the open garage doors. He looked like he wanted to run inside to try to rescue his beloved cars, but the blast of heat kept him back.

'Don't do it!' I told him, just to make sure. 'They're all replaceable. That's why you have insurance!'

Cree took his arm. 'I am so sorry,' she said.

I heard the wail of approaching sirens.

'What happened?' I asked the buzz-cut kid.

'I dunno.' He shrugged. 'Angel must have smelled something. He started barking. That's when I saw the smoke and ran inside to let Mr. Hunt know.'

'I knew Angel would work out,' Mrs.

Hunt said. 'You had better take him inside, though, before he gets too excited.'

Before he eats the firemen, more like it.

'Yes, Ma'am,' the kid said.

Mrs. Hunt followed him to where Angel still barked frantically, and I could hear her praising the dog, saying what a good boy he was, how he deserved a special treat for detecting the fire.

Cree sighed. 'There will be no getting rid of that creature now,' she muttered.

'Maybe Davy will come to his senses,' I said softly.

The Mad Russian strode angrily toward us. Did he want to complain about the disturbance? I wouldn't have put it past him. Instead, though, he pulled off his white chef's hat and fingered it unhappily.

'Am sorry,' he said. 'Is my fault, Mr. Hunt.'

'What!' Davy said, startled.

'Is accident with kerosene. Is smelly. We work behind garage — odor not bother guests there.'

'Kerosene!' I said incredulously. 'What were you doing with *that?*'

'Is for starting fire on charcoals, for grilling of steaks and salmons.'

Davy nodded curtly, lips pressed into a thin white line. 'We will discuss it later.'

'Da.' The Mad Russian moved away from us, still frowning unhappily. Hopefully the caterers had insurance.

Then the police and a fire engine arrived. The Russian and his coworkers bunched to one side, watching grimly.

The firemen got down to business. I had to hand it to them, they worked quickly and had the blaze out in less than five minutes, though they continued to soak the roof and charred spots longer than I thought necessary.

To my surprise, the garage didn't collapse. The back wall and part of the roof were thoroughly burnt, and the vehicles inside covered with soot and sodden ash, but overall it could have been far worse.

Then came half an hour of questioning from police and firemen, all armed with clipboards and report forms. Luckily the Mad Russian took full responsibility for everything.

'Is bad luck,' he kept saying. 'Kerosene spill. Bad luck. Am sorry.'

'I'm not going to think about anything but you until tomorrow,' Davy finally told Cree, turning his back on the garage. 'Insurance can wait!'

'Only an hour until the party starts,' I pointed out. Nobody had been watching the clock, with all the excitement going on. 'We probably need to finish up inside . . . '

Cree looked startled. 'Oh yes! My meatballs!'

'Don't worry about them,' Davy said. 'They weren't sitting out long.'

From behind us, Mrs. Hunt added, 'It's not like there's any *meat* in them to spoil.'

I patted Cree's arm reassuringly. 'I'm sure they're fine.'

Nevertheless, Cree hurried inside. Looking glum, Davy followed, with his mother leaning on his arm and chatting nonstop about not letting anything spoil the party.

'The show must go on!' she said firmly. 'No matter what, the guests must not be disappointed!'

'I think we could all use a drink after that,' Mr. Hunt said from behind me. 'I can make a fresh pitcher of martinis.'

'Hear, hear!' I said. I definitely felt the shakes coming on; I *wanted* that drink; it had been too long . . .

Davy looked devastated. Those cars had meant a lot to him.

'Like the Russian said, Davy, it was just bad luck.' I leaned on his shoulder sympathetically. Then I told him how rude the man had been to me out on the lawn. 'Better get a different catering service for the wedding.'

'I would, but . . . ' He shrugged. 'Mom's been using them for years. They have done her enough favors that we can't possibly replace them now. Dad even sponsored Paolo for membership at our country club.'

Mrs. Hunt said, 'Paolo's a good man. And accidents do happen.'

Suddenly, from the kitchen, Cree screamed. What now? We all hurried the last few steps to the kitchen.

'What's wrong?' Davy asked.

'My ring!' Cree cried. 'It is gone!'

'What!' Davy said.

All the caterers had turned to stare — even the Mad Russian, who had been fussing with the entrees.

'I put it behind the stove while I made the meatballs!' Cree said. 'See? It is not there now!'

I limped over to her. Sure enough, the ring had disappeared.

'Pit?' Davy said helplessly, looking at me.

'It was the Society Bandit!' Mrs. Hunt said. 'I know it!'

I looked from Davy to Cree. Cree wrung her hands. She looked ready to burst into tears.

'Cree's right,' I said. 'I remember her taking it off, then setting it right *there*, behind the burners.' I pointed. There was a faint smudge where the ring had been. I touched it, smelled it. Onion, a hint of garlic, a hint of spearmint ... and something I couldn't quite identify. *Odd.* I had one of those trick memories; I could recall every name, date, fact, and figure I had ever encountered, but I couldn't quite place this scent.

'It was the Society Bandit!' Mrs. Hunt said again. 'Call the police! Robert?'

'I'm here, dear,' Mr. Hunt said, from just behind her.

Cree sobbed, 'Oh, Davy!'

Davy looked uneasy. 'Don't worry, it's insured. We can get a replacement tomorrow — '

'I do *not* want a replacement! I *want* the one you gave me!'

'Where was your dog when this happened?' I asked. Maybe some good could come of it, and Davy would see how useless Angel really was.

'Angel . . . ' Davy muttered. He went to the door and bellowed, 'Oscar!'

'Yes, Mr. Hunt?' came the kid's voice, distant but clear.

'Come to the kitchen!'

'Yes, sir!'

Oscar appeared at the doorway.

'Yes, Mr. Hunt?' he asked. 'You wanted me?'

'My wife's engagement ring is missing.'

'Oh no!' He glanced down at Angel almost guiltily. 'It must have happened while the fire distracted everyone. That

Society Bandit . . . '

'I don't think so,' I said. 'The Society Bandit's *modus operandi* doesn't fit this case. He always strikes during parties, when a lot of people are about. There isn't anyone here yet except family and staff.'

'And *you*,' the kid said, eyes narrowing slightly.

'What's that supposed to mean?' I demanded. Was he accusing *me* of stealing the ring?

'Weren't you the last one out of the kitchen?' he said.

I raised my cane. 'Come here so I can hit you.' I'd had just about enough of him. 'I'm *crippled*, remember? I can't exactly run outside when there's a fire!'

'Drop it, Oscar,' Davy said sharply, stepping between us. 'Pit's not only my oldest friend, he's going to be my best man at the wedding.'

Davy hadn't told me that yet, and I didn't really have time to react beyond an initial silent, 'Wow.' It was quite an honor. And I hadn't been expecting it.

'So what *do* you think, Pit?' Davy

continued. 'You're the genius! What happened to Cree's ring?'

Turning, I limped back to the stove. 'Everyone stop what you're doing!' I called to the caterers. Those not already looking my way turned to face me. 'Don't touch anything. There might be finger-prints.'

'You are crazy man!' said the Mad Russian, taking a half step forward. 'Everyone here leave fingerprints!'

'Shut up,' I told him. 'This particular disaster doesn't concern you. Yet.'

He shut up. But if his glare could have killed, I would have been reduced to a pile of cinders.

My gaze swept over the bowls of ingredients. They hadn't been touched. Then I looked over the half empty bowl of tofu-mixture. Then the baking sheet with the rows of meatballs.

Two of which were missing.

I blinked in surprise. Why would a thief take a diamond ring and two uncooked veggie meatballs?

Angel began to whine almost plain-tively. I glanced at him. He was sniffing the air in the direction of the stove.

'Nice dog,' I said. I picked up a meatball and tossed it to him. He snatched it out of the air and swallowed without chewing. The tail wagged for a second. At least someone liked veggie meatballs with black rice.

'What are you doing?' Cree cried.

'Don't feed him!' Oscar said sharply. 'He's on a structured diet!'

'He likes your meatballs,' I said to Cree, ignoring the kid. 'Two meatballs are missing. What if our thief fed them to Angel?'

'To get him to stop barking,' Davy mused, 'while he stole the ring?'

'No,' said Oscar, folding his hands stubbornly. 'I was with Angel every second after the fire. We didn't see anyone. We weren't in the kitchen at all.'

'Can anyone verify that?' I asked, looking around at the caterers. They shifted, looking from one to another, but none spoke up. I nodded slowly. Hadn't they all been outside watching the fire?

Since I wasn't feeding Angel anymore, he decided to help himself. He jumped up, front legs on the island, and stretched his neck toward the tray.

'Angel! Down!' Oscar said sharply.

Guiltily, it seemed to me, the dog obeyed. He returned to the kid's side and licked Oscar's hand instead ... like it tasted of Cree's meatball mix?

'You did it!' I said to Oscar. 'That's why he's licking your hand!'

He gaped at me. 'No way! I wouldn't feed Angel to get him to cooperate! He already does whatever I say.'

'Then where's the ring?' Davy said.

'I don't know! Go ahead and search me!'

'No ... ' I paused, frowning. He was right. I'd missed something.

What *was* the lingering smell on the counter? Kerosene? *No* ...

Maybe the thief had an accomplice? I glanced at the caterers. The Mad Russian was frowning heavily. But then, that seemed his normal expression.

'I'm not going to stay here and be accused of crimes I didn't commit,' Oscar said angrily. He started for the door. 'Angel, heel!'

'Wait right there,' Davy said severely.

Memories came back . . . my own dog when I had been a boy, a black-and-brown mutt named Max, friendly as anything. When he got sick, we hid pills in bits of ground meat. He swallowed everything without chewing.

Just like Angel had.

'The thief could have fed the ring to the dog,' I said suddenly.

'You walk him, right, Oscar? Easy for you to collect the ring when it comes out the other end.'

Oscar gaped. 'You're crazy!'

'Pit is a genius,' Davy said, 'and if he says you took the ring, I believe him. Cree?' He turned to his fiancée. 'Would you run outside? I think the police are still here working on their report.'

'With pleasure,' she said.

'Wait,' I told her.

Oscar was shaking his head sadly. 'Mr. Hunt,' he said in a quiet voice, 'you're making a huge mistake. I'm not a thief. I help *stop* the bad guys!'

'That ring was worth a small fortune,' I said.

'I make a *lot* of money. I don't *need* to steal. I have dozens of clients.'

'That's true,' said Mrs. Hunt. 'Everyone I know gets their dogs from Oscar. He works miracles with them. Stop this nonsense now and find the real thief!'

'Pit is always right,' Davy said stubbornly.

'So am I!' his mother said.

'If Pit says Oscar stole Cree's ring, I'd bet money he did it.'

I threw two more meatballs to Angel.

'Nice doggie,' I said.

'Would you *stop that*!' Oscar cried. He maneuvered himself between Angel and me. And as he did, I realized he wouldn't feed a ring or raw veggie meatballs to Angel for any amount of money. He really seemed upset by my giving people-food to Angel.

'How do we get the ring out?' Davy asked me.

I shrugged. 'Feed him, then let nature take its course, I guess. Have Oscar wait in your library. We'll know in a few hours whether he's telling the truth.'

Oscar folded his arms and glared. 'And

then I'll expect an apology, Mr. Hunt!'

'Moose?' I said to Davy's father. 'Why don't you show him the way to the library? And keep him company while we wait? Maybe he'd like a martini.'

'I don't drink,' Oscar said sullenly.

That clinched it for me. He had to be a health nut . . . which meant he definitely hadn't fed the ring to Angel. But I still remembered how he'd accused *me* of the crime. Call me petty, but I'd let him sweat it out for a bit.

Where had the ring gone? Maybe Oscar had an accomplice?

'Guard duty, eh?' Davy's father said, grinning. 'Haven't done that since my army days.' He blinked. 'Hey, how'd you know my old nickname! Nobody's called me Moose in thirty years!'

'You told me to call you Moose at our graduation party. We're fraternity brothers, you said.' I paused. 'You *had* been drinking.'

'Robert!' Mrs. Hunt said disapprovingly.

'Uh, off to the library,' he said. He gave me a wink, then patted Cree's hand.

'Don't worry,' he told her. 'It will all work out. True love always finds a way.'

'Thanks, Dad,' Davy said.

Oscar looked at Davy's mother. 'Mrs. Hunt? Can't you make them see reason?'

'I'm sorry, Oscar,' she said. 'Please humor Davy for now. I'm sure he'll make it worth your while when he's proved wrong.'

Oscar continued to argue and insist that he hadn't fed the ring to Angel as Mr. Hunt escorted him out.

Davy drew me aside. 'This party is turning into a real disaster,' he told me unhappily.

'And it's going to get worse,' I said. 'Angel is innocent. And probably Oscar, too. I'd bet money on it.'

'But . . . you just accused Oscar of feeding the ring to him!'

'Yes. It was necessary. Now the real thief will think he's gotten away with it.'

He frowned. 'Do you know who did it?'

'No. But we need to start by eliminating suspects.'

I glanced pointedly at Angel, who sat alone and forgotten beside the door. He was still staring at the island counter and the tray of meatballs, but he hadn't moved a muscle since Oscar made him sit down.

'You're going to question the dog?' Davy asked.

'A good detective starts with the most obvious solution first,' I said in a low voice, so no one else could hear. 'Maybe Oscar is lying. Call a vet. I don't think Angel ate the ring, but you ought to get him X-rayed to make sure.'

Muttering something about insanity, Davy grabbed the wall phone and stomped into the other room. A subdued Cree, being comforted by Mrs. Hunt, excused herself to get dressed for the party.

'Must prepare the food now!' the Mad Russian told me. 'Almost time for party!'

I nodded. 'Go ahead.'

The caterers went back at work, grimly silent now. We only had half an hour till the guests started to arrive, and the fire had put everyone behind schedule.

Since Cree wouldn't have time to cook the meatballs for dinner, I set the bowl of unshaped mix on the floor. Without Oscar here to restrain him, Angel dug right in — ravenously devouring it all, then licking the bowl clean. So much for a special diet. Then I let him finish off the meatballs on the tray.

Why *had* two meatballs disappeared? If Angel hadn't eaten them, who had?

I glanced around the room . . . and my gaze settled on the aluminum tray filled with Swedish meatballs. A mental light came on. Hide a tree in a forest . . . Where else to hide a meatball but in a giant tray of them?

The Mad Russian lifted the Swedish meatballs and hurried for the side door. Grabbing my cane, I limped after him. Could he have done it? Was he now making his getaway?

Out the door, down the steps, and over to the red and white canopy he went, taking long, brisk strides. He never glanced back, completely oblivious to everything and everyone. I paused twenty feet back as he plopped the tray down over a burner, adjusted the low flame, then covered the meatballs with foil.

When he started back to the house, he drew up short.

'No samples!' he said gruffly. 'I tell you already!'

'Cree's engagement ring might be in that tray of meatballs,' I said. Leaning heavily on my cane, I limped forward. My legs ached; I'd been on my feet too much already. God, I needed a drink.

'Impossible!' he said.

'Let me look.'

When he took a deep breath as if to argue, I cut him off.

'If it's in there,' I pointed out, 'you'll be a hero to Davy and Cree. Why not try to save the day for them, instead of making things worse?'

'You accuse *me* of being thief?'

'I know you didn't do it,' I said. 'You were outside all the time. I'm your alibi. I *saw* you there.'

'Very well.' He nodded curtly. 'We look!'

Together we returned to the tray. The Mad Russian peeled back the aluminum foil, and I gazed at layers of meatballs in a creamy brown sauce. One in the back corner — a little larger and much darker — caught my eye immediately.

'That one,' I said, pointing.

'Is burnt!'

The Mad Russian spooned that meatball onto a small paper plate. When he tried to cut it in half, the spoon clinked dully against metal.

'Is ring!' he said wonderingly.

'Yes.'

Taking the spoon from his hand, I pried the meatball apart. Our thief hadn't done a very good job; clearly he wasn't experienced at meatball-making — which ruled out the caterers. But I had already eliminated them as suspects; they had all been outside watching the fire, too.

Then I spotted a single thick brown hair in the middle of the meatball . . . a dog's hair.

I hadn't expected that. I really *had* believed Oscar was innocent. But you can't argue with such damning proof. And suddenly it struck me that the odor in the kitchen — the odor I hadn't been able to identify — was *dog*. Angel had a very musky, very doggy odor. Whoever

213

had shaped the meatballs around the ring must have been petting Angel . . .

Which meant Oscar. No one else could have gotten close enough.

I glanced up when the side door to the house banged open. Davy trotted out, phone in hand.

'I reached an emergency vet,' he said, joining us, 'and he says he can X-ray Angel immediately. I'm going to drive over now — '

'Don't bother,' I said. 'We just found Cree's ring.'

'What! Where?'

I pointed at the meatball as I explained. Davy reached for it, but I caught his hand.

'No you don't — that's evidence!' I said. 'Get Cree and your mother. They should both be there when we confront Oscar.'

'All right. What about the police?'

'We don't want a scandal to ruin your engagement party.'

He nodded. 'Right, it's best to take care of it quietly.'

'Of course.' I turned to the Mad

Russian, leaning heavily on my cane. 'Carry the plate inside for me, please?'

★　★　★

Five minutes later, we were all assembled in the library. It was a pleasant wood-paneled room with floor-to-ceiling bookshelves on three of the walls, all filled with expensive first editions that Davy's interior decorator had selected for their fancy leather bindings rather than their content. Cree stood to one side, with Davy's arm around her shoulders. She had been crying but was trying not to show it. Mr. and Mrs. Hunt stood by the drink cart, sipping martinis. Mrs. Hunt had her ever-present cigarette and a haze slowly settled over the room.

I came last through the door, behind the Mad Russian. Mr. Hunt handed me a vodka martini unasked, which I downed in one gulp. Not strong enough, but it would do for starters. The pain had spread from my legs to my back.

Oscar perched alone on the edge of the red leather sofa, knees pressed tightly together, arms folded, looking small and sad and distinctly uncomfortable.

'We found the ring,' I told him, 'in one of the Swedish meatballs.'

'Then you know I'm innocent.' He started to rise.

'Sit back down!' I said. 'You left a hair in the middle of the meatball. Take a look!'

I nodded to the Mad Russian, who handed the paper plate to Oscar. Oscar glanced at it, then looked away. He said nothing.

'Care to confess?' I asked.

'It's not my hair.'

'It's Angel's,' I said.

He shrugged. 'Dogs shed. Hair gets everywhere. It doesn't prove anything.'

'It proves that whoever made the meatball didn't wash his hands after petting Angel.'

He shrugged again. 'Or the hair blew in. Or you planted it there.'

'Let's start at the beginning,' I said. 'Maybe we can make sense of everything.' I crossed to the drink cart and refilled my martini glass with two fingers of single malt whiskey from a crystal decanter. I sipped slowly, drawing out the suspense. 'I bet you planned on filling a plate from the buffet. You counted on being able to spot the meatball you had made yourself — it was a bit larger than the others, and since it was made with black rice, it looked burnt. The caterers wouldn't have served it to any of the guests.' I turned to the Mad Russian. 'Isn't that right?'

'*Da,*' he said. 'Burnt meatballs always left in pan.'

Davy said, 'What do you have to say for yourself, Oscar?'

'I wouldn't eat at your party — I'm a vegan!'

'Besides, what if someone else picked that meatball?' Davy's father asked.

I said, 'If one of the guests *did* take it, there are twenty-odd people here catering the party. The police would never be able to pin the crime on any one of them. Angel's hair really *is* the only clue.'

'And it's meaningless!' Oscar said. He looked at Mrs. Hunt, the one sympathetic face in the crowd. 'Can I go now?'

'No,' I said.

'Pit . . . ' Davy said in a warning tone. 'Don't you think this has gone on long enough?'

If it wasn't a crime of greed, what could it be? Oscar had a lot to lose in stealing a ring. What motive could be greater than money? Love? Power?

'Our criminal mastermind left almost nothing to chance,' I mused aloud, trying to put the pieces together. And when my gaze settled on Mrs. Hunt, suddenly things began to click into place. This crime *wasn't* about money. The ring's value was incidental. It was all about power. *Family* power. 'Isn't that right, Mrs. Hunt?'

'What?' she said, clearly startled. 'Why — er — yes, I suppose so.'

'Especially,' I said, 'since that criminal mastermind is *you*.'

She gaped. 'What — ?'

'Connie?' said a bewildered Mr. Hunt.

'Mom?' Davy said in a warning tone. 'What have you done?'

Oscar sighed and grinned and looked relieved all at the same time. It must have been quite a burden off his back.

'He caught you, Mrs. Hunt,' he said simply, and I knew I'd guessed correctly. The kid probably hadn't wanted to take the ring in the first place. But he owed a lot of his business to Mrs. Hunt and her referrals.

'Don't bother to deny it,' I said to Davy's mother. 'When there aren't any definite clues, you have to look at motive. And you're the only one here with a real motive!'

'What are you talking about?' Davy's father demanded, looking from me to her and back again.

Davy understood, though. 'Mom hates Cree's engagement ring, and she wanted us to use Grandmother's instead.'

I added, 'What better way than to swipe the old one, blame it on the Society Bandit, and make herself a heroine by producing a replacement at the last second? I bet she has that extra engagement ring in her pocketbook *right now.*'

'What nonsense!' Mrs. Hunt said.

Mr. Hunt snatched the pocketbook from her arm, opened it over her protests, and rummaged around inside. Pulling out a small red jewelry box, he popped back the lid. A large diamond surrounded by sapphires glinted. It was quite a ring.

'Connie!' barked Mr. Hunt.

'Oh, all right!' she snapped. 'I don't know how he figured it out, but I made Oscar run back inside and take the ring when I saw Cree leave it on the counter!' She turned to Davy and Cree, anger making her voice shake. 'You two spoiled brats don't understand how *important* our family's traditions are! Three generations of Hunt women have gotten engaged wearing that ring — '

'Get out,' Davy said, in a voice so quiet I knew he was barely containing the fury. 'You're no longer welcome at our wedding, Mother.'

'What!' she cried.

'Now Davy,' I said patiently, 'you know you don't mean that. Your mother stole the ring because she cares *so much* for you and for Cree.'

Cree put her hand on Davy's arm. 'Your mother is right,' she said simply. 'It was selfish of me not to take her ring to begin with. Mother Hunt,' she said, crossing to the drink cart, 'I did not realize it meant so much to you. Of course, I will wear your mother's ring . . . and proudly.'

'Cree!' Davy said. 'Don't do it!'

'Thank you,' Mr. Hunt whispered. He looked like someone had just hit him in the stomach with a baseball bat.

Cree took the ring box from his fingers, removed the ring, and slipped it onto her right index finger. It looked stunning when she held it up for all to see.

'I had it sized for you,' Mrs. Hunt said. 'Isn't it lovely, my dear?'

'Come, Davy,' Cree said, taking his elbow and pulling him toward the door. 'You still have to dress for the party.'

She was a stronger woman than I had ever figured. And with a noble streak, too . . . sacrificing her own pride for the sake of Davy's family.

Not that Mrs. Hunt deserved such nobility. But Davy certainly did.

When Davy and Cree were gone, I took charge. That's the sort of thing a best man would do.

'You had better get back to your work,'

I said to the Mad Russian. 'The guests will be here soon. Everything has to be ready.'

'*Da,*' he said, and off he went.

I retrieved the plate with the meatball and its ring from Oscar. He gulped as he looked me in the eye.

'You're fired,' I told him. 'Take your dog and get out. I don't want either of you menacing Davy and Cree's guests tonight. Or ever again.'

'Uh . . . ' He glanced at Mrs. Hunt, who gave a curt nod. Then he bolted for the door.

When he was gone, I turned to Davy's parents and folded my arms. Mr. Hunt looked sick. Mrs. Hunt stared into the distance, puffing steadily on her cigarette.

'I trust you realize how much Cree loves Davy. For her to make a sacrifice like that . . . well, she's a better person than I am. I never would have forgiven you.'

Turning, I limped for the door, pausing just long enough to scoop up the decanter of whiskey. My reward for a job well done.

As the door clicked shut behind me, I heard Mrs. Hunt begin to cry. Maybe there was hope for her yet.

I went straight to the kitchen, washed the original engagement ring clean of black rice and herbs, and slipped it into my pocket. I'd give it back to Davy after the party.

Angel and Oscar had both vanished, of course. And all the caterers had gone out to the canopy.

When the doorbell rang, I straightened my tie, slicked back my hair with one hand, and limped out to greet the first of the guests. We still had a party to run.

5

Horse Pit

When the telephone rang, I rolled over
and squinted at it. *Not again*. Why couldn't
people leave me alone? If I wanted to sit
in my apartment and drink until the pain
stopped, was that too much to ask?

Sighing, I fumbled the receiver to my
ear. Probably telemarketers. Best to get it
over with.

'Hullo?' I rasped. My mouth tasted like
day-old bread.

'Pit?' It was David Hunt, my only
remaining friend. We had been in the
same fraternity in college. I hadn't heard
from Davy in a couple of weeks, so the
call was due.

Groaning, I managed to sit up. My
head throbbed and my bones ached; the
room tilted out from under me. Where
had I put that bottle of Jack Daniels?
Probably somewhere under the covers,

hopefully with the cap still on. Booze was the only thing that blunted the pain from my ruined legs. And it had the welcome side-effect of slowing my always-racing mind.

'Hi, Davy,' I managed to say in an almost normal voice.

'You up?' he asked.

'Kinda.' I yawned. 'What time is it?'

'Midnight.'

That brought me fully awake. Davy was a morning person; he rarely stayed up past ten o'clock. Something must have happened. Something bad for him to call this late.

'What's wrong?' I demanded. 'Are you and Cree all right?'

'We're fine. It's just . . . I bought a race horse!'

I blinked. '*What?*'

'A race horse. Pretty cool, huh? His name's Bailey's Final Call, and he's won several stakes races over the last year.'

'Are you insane?' I rubbed my crusty eyes, wishing I'd never awakened, wishing I'd never been born. 'You called me at midnight to say you bought a *horse?*'

'Yep!'

'You barely know which end to feed!'

'That's what jockeys are for.'

I thought he was joking. I hoped he was joking.

Davy went on, 'Actually, I'm one-fifth owner. A bunch of us formed a mini-syndicate. Opportunity of a lifetime, and all that.'

Since Davy was already worth upwards of fifty million, if anyone could make a profit from a horse, he could. He had a Midas touch.

But why call me? I had no interest in horses. And why so late? Something didn't fit.

Gingerly, I eased my feet to the floor. 'What are your plans for this unfortunate creature?' I asked. Flicking on the light, I felt around my faded blue bedspread. Where *had* that bottle gone?

Davy said, 'A few more races, then we put him out to stud.'

'Is there money in that?' Maybe Bailey's Final Call wasn't so unfortunate.

'For a champion? You'd better believe it. I think — '

I found my Jack Daniels . . . cap on, but empty. So much for that. I added it to the growing pile of empties in the corner as Davy nattered on about his horse, but I only half listened. I'd have to recycle everything soon.

' — already worth more than a hundred thousand a year in stud fees,' Davy was saying. 'There will be more — lots more — if he keeps on winning.'

I whistled. 'The sex trade really pays.' What was the average lifespan of a horse, anyway? Twenty years? Thirty? At a hundred thousand a year . . . or more . . .

'It pays for horses, anyway.'

'And what did this creature cost?'

'A lot.'

'Davy . . . ' A warning note crept into my voice. 'I know you're calling because you want my help with something, so don't get cute. How much did you spend?'

He laughed, but uncertainly, as if he had something to hide. That sent up more warning flags.

'Spill it!' I ordered.

'Okay, okay. We each chipped in two

hundred thousand.'

I gasped. 'You spent a million dollars on *one horse?* What were you thinking?'

'Bailey *is* a champion.' He sounded defensive. 'It seemed like a good idea at the time.'

'But now you think you were ripped off.'

A confirming silence followed. My doubts turned into a horrible premonition.

'Davy-boy?' I said.

'Let's say . . . I have a bad feeling. Will you help me or not?'

'I know nothing about racing. I know less about horses.'

'You're the smartest guy I know, Pit. If anyone can spot a scam, you can.'

'I'm flattered, but you need an expert. How about Dick Francis? That guy knows crime *and* horses. With your money, I bet you could rent him for an afternoon.'

'Get serious, Pit. We've already had two vets and a trainer look Bailey over. They say he's sound of hoof and heart. By all accounts, he's the real deal.'

'Then be happy. You got a bargain, right?'

'I don't know.' He hesitated. 'I can't put my finger on it. But something's wrong. Bailey sold way too cheap.'

'A million dollars isn't cheap.'

'For an investment that's going to yield three to ten million in profit, that's rock bottom. He's worth at least double what we paid.'

'People find bargains all the time. I don't see your problem.'

'Trust me on this.'

'If you're getting cold feet, sell him off and count your blessings. And your profits.'

'I can't. My partners plan on running Bailey in the Kentucky Derby. If I dump my share and something *is* wrong with him, everyone will think I found out and deliberately stuck my buddies. Lawsuits, ruined friendships, nasty gossip . . . '

'Better to go down with — er — the horse?'

'Exactly. So what do you say, Pit?'

'No.' It didn't add up.

'Why not?'

'Because you aren't telling me the whole truth.' I knew him too well. 'Your story doesn't match your personality — or your finances. So have fun with your pet, and leave me out of it.'

I hung up. Did I have another bottle of whiskey in the kitchen cabinet? Yesterday hazed over in my mind. I could have finished it in bed. But maybe not. I hobbled in to see.

The phone rang . . . and rang . . .

Nothing in the cabinet but a single can of tomato soup. Which meant I'd need to get dressed tomorrow and walk to the state store for more. God, I hated leaving my apartment.

Still the phone rang. Fifteen times. Twenty.

He wasn't going away. And, if I didn't answer, he'd drive out and bang on my apartment door. He'd done it before.

At last I grabbed the receiver. 'Yes?'

'What do you mean,' he said as though I'd never hung up on him, 'about my story not matching my personality?'

'Or your finances.'

'Yeah. That, too.'

I sighed as I sat at my tiny kitchen table. 'I have more than a vague idea of your net worth, Davy. Two hundred thousand is pocket change. You probably have that much lying around your house.'

'Uh . . . maybe,' he said. 'But if I did, I'd keep it locked in a safe.'

'Now,' I continued, warming up, 'let's assume you bought Bailey on a lark. You're rich; he's a new toy. Your golf club pals are pitching in, too. But suddenly you panic. Why?'

'You tell me,' he said.

'I can only think of one reason. Buying the horse became a point of honor.' I paused, and the truth came to me like the final piece of a puzzle snapping into place. 'Cree told you not to buy Bailey's Final Call, didn't she?'

Cree was Davy's fiancée, a stunning model — and not the bubblehead you'd expect from her *Sports Illustrated* swimsuit photos. I liked her a lot. In the last year, she had cured Davy of most of his playboy ways — Bailey's Final Call notwithstanding.

In a quiet voice, Davy said, 'You're right. Cree told me not to join the syndicate. But I did it anyway. On paper, it looks like it's a moneymaker. Better be, or I'll never hear the end of it. But now I'm getting a funny — '

'Maybe it's guilt,' I said softly. After my nervous breakdown, I'd seen enough shrinks to last a lifetime. They had all talked to me in the same soothing tone. 'Maybe you're looking for a way to get out of the deal for Cree's sake. After all, you don't want to fight with her.'

'Something *is* wrong with that horse. I *know* it. You've got to help, Pit.'

'But I can barely tell a fetlock from a furlong!'

'Don't make me beg.'

Of all things, a race horse. But I couldn't let my friend down. He was the only one who kept in touch, kept pushing me to leave my apartment, get outside and actually *think*. I would have drunk myself to death by now without him.

'All right,' I said. 'I'll do what I can. Where are you keeping this refugee from the glue factory?'

'Black Fox Farm in Buckston. That's in — '

'I know, Bucks County.' About an hour

north of Philadelphia. Lots of old money, lots of horses.

'I'm driving out tomorrow,' Davy said. 'Pick you up at eight?'

I muttered something about ungodly hours, but he laughed.

'Don't forget, dress for a farm.' He hung up.

Against my will, odd bits of information about horses began popping into my head. I had one of those trick brains: I could recall every name, face, fact, and figure I had ever encountered while sober. To my surprise, lists of Kentucky Derby winners (and losers), Belmont Stakes purses, and even old episodes of *Mr. Ed* and *My Friend Flicka* from a misspent childhood in front of the TV bubbled up. I knew more about horses than I'd thought.

Cursing Davy and his new toy, I levered myself out of my chair and limped around the apartment, bagging empty whiskey bottles, picking out clothes. So much for sleep. I'd never get any rest now.

★ ★ ★

The next morning, Davy roared up to my apartment building in his shiny silver BMW convertible, music blaring from the satellite radio. He owned half a dozen cars, and he'd chosen my personal favorite despite the slate-gray sky threatening rain.

Leaning hard on the railing, I worked my way down four short steps to the sidewalk. It promised to be a hot, uncomfortable, muggy day; typical late June weather in Philadelphia.

Davy reached over and opened the door for me. When I glared, he grinned his perfect smile and touched the brim of his green *Sports Illustrated* cap in salute. God, I hate morning people. They're so damn *cheerful*.

'You owe me big for this.'

'I'll name my first kid after you.'

Snorting, I eased my way inside. He had already put the seat back as far as it would go. Tentatively, I stretched my legs out. I could endure the cramped space for an hour or so.

The moment I slammed the door, Davy accelerated into light rush-hour traffic. Row houses streamed past. I buckled my safety belt and closed my eyes. The familiar smells of Philly's Northwood section — soft pretzels from the street corner vendors, already-baking asphalt, diesel bus exhaust — washed over me. Three blocks later, we turned onto Roosevelt Boulevard's express lanes and sped up, heading north.

'Want to stop for coffee?' Davy asked.

'Are you trying to poison me?'

'You can't live on alcohol alone.'

'One group of medieval monks lived on nothing *but* beer.'

'Really?'

'They brewed it so thick, it became almost a bread. Beer and pizza gets me cheese and tomato sauce, too. Covers all my food groups.'

'Not healthy.'

'Tell you what, get us there in forty-five minutes instead of an hour and you can buy me lunch at the restaurant of your choice.'

Grinning, he floored the accelerator. He probably had visions of Salad Alley dancing through his head.

* * *

We flew until we left the city limits. Then we hit construction delays and crawled the last twenty miles. By the time Davy turned off Route 202 and onto a rutted gravel driveway, we had been driving almost two hours. Pains wracked my body, from the steel pins in my legs to my overly compressed spinal cord to the knotted-up muscles in my neck and shoulders. Fortunately I had taken half a dozen aspirin before leaving my apartment. Those, plus the Motrin I had dry-swallowed on the road, made my pains almost bearable. I *really* needed something alcoholic.

Finally Davy said, 'There it is.'

I sat up straighter. A small, weathered sign said BLACK FOX FARM.

We turned onto a private road and cruised between two ivy-covered stone gateposts — the gates themselves were missing — then crossed a dense line of poplars and white birches, lush in their summer greenness.

Rounding a corner, the farm came into view. To the right, inside a pasture with a split-rail fence, six brown-and-white horses raised their heads to gaze at us. To the left, in an exercise ring, a girl of nine or ten in an English riding habit sat astride a lanky brown horse with a white nose.

Two men stood watching the girl. One was thin and grizzled, with bib overalls and a Phillies baseball cap. The other was burly and gray-haired with a ponytail. Ponytail-man frowned as Davy neared.

'Is that girl riding Bailey?' I asked.

'Uh . . . ' Davy squinted. 'I'm not sure.'

'You *do* know what your horse looks like?'

'He's brown.'

I rolled my eyes.

Directly ahead sat a sprawling Victorian-style farmhouse. It had a fresh coat of white paint, but the roof and front porch sagged, and I got an impression of benign neglect. Picturesque oak trees flanked the house, half obscuring a pair of ancient red barns with fieldstone foundations. Both barns had Pennsylvania Dutch hex signs under the eaves. Any watercolor artist would have drooled.

The man with the ponytail left the exercise ring and stalked in our direction.

He looked quite annoyed.

'Who's that?' I asked.

'Mitch Goldsmith. We bought Bailey from him.'

'Did you tell him we were coming?'

Davy grinned and waved to Mitch. Through his teeth, he said to me, 'Why should I? It's *my* horse!'

'Only twenty percent.'

Cruising past the exercise ring, Davy parked next to a battered silver horse-van and a bright red Sebring convertible. As he cut the engine, I popped my door and heaved my feet out. White-hot fires surged the length of my legs. Gasping, I paused to knead and massage my calves through ridges of scar-tissue. It took a minute, but the pain receded.

By the time I struggled to my feet, Mitch had reached the other side of the car. His stained navy-blue polo shirt had BLACK FOX FARM stitched across the right breast in silver thread.

'Yo, Mitch,' Davy said cheerfully. He tossed his baseball cap onto the dashboard and ran his fingers through his short blond hair. 'How's Bailey this morning?'

'We don't like drop-in visitors,' Mitch said. 'It upsets the routine.'

'Don't think of us as visitors, think of us as family.' Davy flashed his perfect smile. 'We're all in this together, right . . . ? As long as we're paying you to train Bailey.'

'Care to make introductions?' I asked from across the car.

'Oh, sorry. Pit, this is Mitch Goldsmith, Bailey's trainer and *former* owner. Mitch, Pit Geller.'

'Hello,' I said. I limped around Davy's BMW, shifting my cane to my left hand and offering Mitch my right. Time to play peacemaker. 'Pleased to meet you, sir.'

He nodded brusquely. 'Call me Mitch.'

I learn a lot about a man in the first seconds of our initial meeting. Pity, revulsion, even outright fear — I've gotten it all since my accident. Pity gets me seats on crowded trains. Revulsion goes usually wears off with the realization that limps aren't contagious. Fear, though, never ends.

Mitch paid no notice to my handicap. He shook hands without hesitation, grip firm but not painful. His palms and fingers had plenty of calluses. Clearly this was no gentleman of leisure. I took an instant liking to him.

'Did I catch your name right?' he asked. 'Pit?'

'A college nickname.' I pulled a sour face. 'Davy won't stop using it, much as I'd like him to. Call me Peter.'

Mitch raised his eyebrows. 'You went to school together?'

'Don't let him fool you,' I said, lowering my voice. We were both thirty-one, but the years hadn't been kind to me. 'Hair dye and plastic surgery did wonders for him. We're both from the class of '75.'

'Pit!' Davy protested.

'Okay, okay. It's really the class of '73. I'm vain about my age, too.' I gave Mitch a wink, and he grinned.

Davy tried to say something, but only managed exasperated noises. Mitch studied him with new interest. Probably wondering whether Davy really could be that old.

'Anyway,' Davy said, giving me a dirty look, 'we were in the neighborhood, and I thought we'd watch Bailey run.'

Mitch glanced at his watch. 'Too late. Bailey finished five minutes ago. You can watch him cool down, I guess.'

'Where do you train him?' I asked.

Mitch waved at someplace beyond the barns. 'It's a five-minute walk. We have fifty acres here, which includes a small track. Follow the path behind the house if you want to see it.'

'Another time.' My legs weren't up to it; I needed more time to recover from the car ride.

'Why aren't *you* training Bailey?' Davy demanded.

'Do I *look* like a jockey?' Mitch gave him a withering glare. 'I weigh a hundred pounds too much. My stepson is with him this morning. Don't worry, Bailey will be ready for the Derby.' He turned toward the exercise ring, paused, glanced back at me. 'Missy just made some pink lemonade. Might as well have a glass while you wait.'

'Thanks.' I would have preferred something stronger, but at least he hadn't offered water.

'That would be great,' Davy said.

'Sure.' Mitch headed for the house. Davy and I stood in silence till he was out of earshot.

'Well?' Davy asked.

'Definitely the criminal type,' I said. 'Pink lemonade . . . it's fiendish!'

Davy punched me in the arm — hard.

'Hey! Ow!' Davy didn't believe in coddling cripples, either. Another reason I liked him so much.

'That's for the hair dye and plastic surgery,' he said.

'What do you expect, dragging me out here for nothing?'

'I'm serious, Pit.'

'Me too. Look at this place! It's falling apart.' I pointed with my cane. 'The house needs a new roof. The paint is a cheap, cosmetic fix. Ditto for both barns. The porch is collapsing. You're looking at eighty or ninety thousand for basic repairs. On top of that, he's got his own kid exercising Bailey rather than a pro. What does it add up to?'

'They need a good contractor?'

'They're broke. Mitch must have lucked out and gotten a champion racehorse, and he's cashing out because he can't afford to maintain the family farm any other way.'

Davy paused. 'You think so?'

'There's a reason horse racing attracts millionaires. Mitch is out of his league.'

'Hmm.' Davy stared into the distance. He'd have to work it out for himself.

A minute later, Mitch reappeared carrying a pair of cheap plastic lawn chairs. He set them up in the shade of one of the oak trees and beckoned us over.

'Might as well relax while we wait for Bailey,' I said, limping forward.

'Yeah. I guess.' Davy sounded more reserved than usual. No doubt disappointed that his conspiracy theory had fizzled.

'Take a load off, Peter,' Mitch said. 'You too, Hunt. Missy will be right out with lemonade.'

'Thanks.' I sagged into the closest seat and balanced my cane across my knees. Much better.

Behind me, the house door slammed. I half turned and spotted a thin woman with curly black hair headed our way. She wore a bright pink housedress with horses embroidered around the hem, and she carried a vintage '50s-style red plastic tray with a matching set of plastic glasses.

'Don't stand there,' she called to Mitch. She had a definite South Jersey accent. 'Bring one of those little tables for our guests!'

'Yes, Missy.' Mitch trotted around the house again. I chuckled. His wife was a force to be reckoned with.

I struggled to my feet.

'Pleased to meet you, ma'am,' I said.

'Don't you 'ma'am' me!' she said. If her hands had been free, she would have been gesturing and tsk-tsking. 'I'm not your grandmother!'

'Yes, uh, Missy?'

'You must be Peter?'

'Peter Geller, yes.'

Mitch sprinted back around the side of the house. He didn't have a table.

'Call Doc Christiansen, Missy!' he shouted. 'Bailey's down!' Turning, he dashed out of sight.

Davy and I exchanged panicked looks.

'Go!' I told him. He sprinted after Mitch.

'Here, Peter.' Missy thrust the tray into my hands, then rushed back to the house.

I set Missy's tray on the seat of my chair, then followed Davy. I rounded the building to find a brown horse with a white star on his forehead and two white front feet lying on his side between the barns. His legs twitched faintly. A slender boy, perhaps sixteen or seventeen, lay across the animal's neck, keeping him on the ground. Mitch knelt by Bailey's head, stroking his nose and whispering soft words.

Davy stood to one side, arms folded, helpless. This had to be his worst financial nightmare. Never mind that an animal might be injured or dying.

'Missy's calling your vet,' I said, panting hard, legs on the verge of buckling.

Bailey jerked twice, then lay still. Too still. Mitch rose slowly, face white.

'Doesn't matter now,' he said, and his voice cracked. 'He's . . . he's dead. Bailey's dead.'

'No!' The kid clutched at the horse,

fingers knotting in his mane. He managed to hold back tears.

Davy and I exchanged a glance. He had an I-told-you-so expression. But I couldn't believe Mitch would set us up. His reaction — and the kid's — felt real.

A distant *crack* echoed across the farm. Mitch staggered. An odd look came over his face. He opened his mouth, but no words came out. The silver lettering on his shirt turned crimson.

'Mitch?' I said, not quite comprehending.

He slid to his knees. Blood flecked his lips and dribbled down his chin. He tried to speak. A heartbeat later, he fell face-first into the dirt.

'Get down!' I shouted, shoving Davy to the ground behind the horse.

'What — ?' Davy began.

'Sniper!' I said.

Mitch's son gaped at us. I reached over, grabbed his shirt, and dragged him across the horse with more strength than I knew I had. I shoved his head to the dirt path.

'Keep down, kid!'

'But — ' The boy struggled to get to his

father, but I leaned hard and kept him in place. Thin as I was, I still outweighed him by thirty or forty pounds.

'Lie still,' I snapped. No way was he standing up. 'We'll get help. Davy — '

'Y-yes.' He yanked his cell phone from its belt-clip and dialed 911.

'Is that what happened to Bailey?' I asked the boy. I shook him to make him focus. 'Was Bailey shot?'

'I — I don't know,' he cried. 'He collapsed — couldn't stand up — '

Davy reached an emergency operator and explained our situation. He listened, repeated himself, listened again, then lowered the phone.

'The police want us to stay down,' he reported. 'They're on their way — and they've called an ambulance for Mitch.'

'Good.' I looked at the boy. 'What's your name?'

'Bobby,' he said, eyes wide.

'Bobby, listen. I have to ask you something important before the police get here.' There was no easy way to put it. 'This horse — he isn't Bailey's Final Call, is he?'

Bobby stared. 'Of course he is. I've known him his whole life. You can't mistake the star on his forehead or his two white socks.'

'Okay.' I believed the kid. But it didn't make sense. Why shoot a champion horse? And why shoot Mitch? Common sense said *Mitch* should be the criminal, not the victim here.

★ ★ ★

I have to give the local police credit. Within two minutes of Davy's call, I heard the wail of approaching sirens. The sniper must have heard them, too. I counted to twenty — time enough for him to make his getaway — then rose on unsteady legs. Nobody shot me. I scanned the distant trees before motioning Davy and Bobby up.

'Tell the ambulance driver where we are,' I ordered Bobby. He took off running.

Davy continued talking on his cell phone, telling the police what was going on. He looked stunned. No help there.

I rolled Mitch onto his back and brushed

dirt from his cheeks and forehead.

'Hey?' I asked. 'Mitch? Can you hear me?'

His eyes opened. They had a glassy sheen, but focused on my face. Then he began to cough, and from deep in his chest came a liquid gurgle. That couldn't be good.

'Hang on,' I said. I squeezed his limp hand. 'You're going to be okay.'

He turned his head slightly. His blood-flecked lips moved.

'Tell . . . ' he breathed.

I bent close.

'Fifi . . . Dows . . . ' His voice trailed off.

'Mitch?' I slapped his cheeks gently, but he had passed out.

Tell Fifi Dows? Who was she? And tell her what?

The back door of the house banged open, and Missy stepped out with a phone to her ear. From her expression, she hadn't heard a thing. She probably had their vet on the line.

She looked from the dead horse to me to Mitch. Then she dropped the phone and screamed.

* ★ *

Things got weird after that. An ambulance . . . police cars . . . flashing lights . . . Missy sobbing . . .

My eyesight narrowed into a kind of tunnel vision. I moved through an unreal haze as bits of conversation, out-of-focus faces, and pulsing red and white lights all jumbled together. A steady thrumming, like rain on a metal roof, filled my ears. I might have been a passenger in someone else's body.

Panic attack. As though in a dream, part of me diagnosed the problem with clinical precision. It had happened too many times before to count. But not this bad. Not in a long, long time. Not since New York.

A woman shoved a microphone into my face. I mumbled answers.

No, I don't know who fired the shots.

No, I don't know anything about Mitch Goldsmith.

No, I don't own Bailey's Final Call.

At one point a young-faced officer with a shaved head and Marine Corps tattoos on his forearms sat with me on the rear bumper of an ambulance. Someone had draped a blanket around my shoulders. I clutched my cane to my chest. I wanted to close my eyes and shut down, but people kept talking and talking and nudging me to respond.

'You did good,' he said, patting my shoulder. 'Don't worry, Pete, we'll get to the bottom of everything.'

'No,' I said numbly. 'No, you won't.'

'What makes you say that?'

'It was a very professional job.'

★ ★ ★

The next thing I knew, I lay in the back seat of Davy's BMW.

Night had fallen. Through the open roof, I stared up at an illuminated blue-and-yellow Best Western motel sign.

Davy must have registered us. He half carried, half dragged me into a room. I crawled into a queen-sized bed, pulled the covers over myself, and passed out.

★ ★ ★

Sometime later, a door squeaked open and hot morning sunlight splashed across my face. I crawled out of my mental hole. Sitting up, I shaded my eyes with a trembling hand and squinted into brightness.

Davy stood silhouetted in the doorway. He hefted a pair of plastic grocery bags onto the round table by the window before turning in my direction.

'Feeling better?'

'No.' I managed to sit up.

'You're talking. That's good. You're pretty freaky when you go non-verbal.'

'I need a drink.'

'Here.' He rummaged around in one of the grocery bags, then tossed a can of Diet Dr. Pepper onto the bed beside me.

I stared at it. 'You have a cruel sense of humor.'

'There's ice in the bucket by the sink. Glasses, too. Drink up.'

'I want whiskey.'

'You're on the clock, Pit. No alcohol.'

'I said I'd look at Bailey. He's dead. Take me home.'

'We aren't leaving. I want to know who killed my horse.'

'Only twenty percent yours.' I paused. 'What about Mitch? Is he okay?'

'No.' His frown deepened. 'The bullet nicked his heart, poor guy. He didn't make it to the hospital.'

I flashed back to the farm. The *crack* of the rifle. The way Mitch fell. Something faintly wrong tickled at the back of my mind, but I couldn't quite place it. Later, maybe.

I said, 'And what about Bailey?'

'Focus, Pit. I already told you he's dead.'

'But was he shot?'

He blinked. 'Uh . . . I never thought to ask. I just assumed, since Mitch . . . '

'Find out. I'm betting he wasn't.'

'Why?'

'I only heard one shot.'

In my head, I ran through our visit from the moment our car pulled into the driveway. I hadn't heard anything unusual before Mitch rounded the corner of the house. Nor had the sniper tried to shoot anyone after Mitch. Could Mitch have been his only target?

Davy said, 'We have to stop at the

police station this morning. They want us to sign the statements we made yesterday. They'll know what killed Bailey.'

'Okay.' A statement? What had I said?

He returned to his shopping bags. 'Here. You'll want this, too.'

He tossed a bottle of generic aspirin next to the Diet Dr. Pepper. At last something useful. While I fumbled with the shrink-wrap, he pulled out mouthwash, toothpaste and toothbrushes, deodorant, packages of generic white underwear, soy protein bars, a couple of cheap-looking gray tee-shirts, and a copy of the *Bucks County Gazette*.

'I'll take the paper,' I said.

'Here.' He handed it over.

Bailey had made the front page: HORSE FARM SNIPER STRIKES! screamed a huge headline. The picture showed Mitch holding Bailey by his halter. Unfortunately, the article offered the barest of facts, but little interested me beyond the fairly impressive list of races Bailey had won.

I flipped through the rest of the *Gazette*, ignoring articles like 'Severe Drought Warnings Bring Water Restrictions,' 'Police

254

Corruption Alleged,' and 'Arsonist Sought in Bar Blaze' as irrelevant. The obituaries made no mention of Mitch Goldsmith, either. We'd have to pick up the next edition. I wanted to know more about Mitch, a lot more.

At last I lowered the paper. 'What next?'

'There's an outlet village down the road,' Davy said, 'but it's not open yet. We can get clean clothes later. In the meantime . . .'

He tossed me one of the gray tee-shirts. It said NEW HOPE, PENNSYLVANIA in neon green letters.

Great. We'd look like tourists.

★ ★ ★

We reached the police station two hours later. Davy pulled into a spot next to the same bright red Sebring convertible I'd seen at Mitch's place. 'HRSKYD' read the license plate. 'Horse Kid'? Probably Mitch's car. Missy must be here.

Davy strolled inside, introduced himself at the front window, and asked for Detective Nuñes. I tried to remember Nuñes, but drew a blank.

'She's with someone,' the officer behind the window replied. His nametag said L. WEINSTEIN. He pointed with his pen toward a line of gray plastic chairs. 'Take a seat. I'll call you when she's free.'

'Thanks.' Davy led the way.

A kid slouched in one of the chairs, head down, watching music videos on an iPod. When he raised his head, I recognized Mitch's son, Bobby.

'Hi,' he said, voice flat. He pulled out his earbuds.

Davy gave a 'Yo' and a nod.

'Hi.' I motioned Davy toward the far end of the line of chairs. He played along and went off by himself. 'Do you remember me?' I asked Bobby. 'Peter Geller.'

'Sure.'

'I'm sorry about what happened.' I settled onto the chair next to him. My hands had begun to tremble, not nerves but a deep, dull pain. I needed a drink to steady myself.

'Thanks. What happened to you?'

'Got run over by a New York taxi. Years ago.'

'No, I meant yesterday.'

He must have seen me shutting down. 'A panic attack. I get them when I'm stressed out.' I shrugged, cleared my throat. 'Anyway, have they arrested anyone yet?'

'No. They keep saying the investigation is ongoing.'

'How is your mother?'

'At my aunt's house. She's not taking it very well.'

I made sympathetic noises.

'How about Fifi?'

He blinked. 'Who?'

'I thought you might know her.' It had been worth a try. *Tell Fifi Dows.* First, I had to find her.

I went on, 'What about Bailey. Do you know what happened to him?'

Bobby shrugged, face tightening. 'He died.'

'Shot?'

'No. At least, I don't think so. I didn't see any blood.'

'Did he stumble? What happened?'

'I was walking him back to the ring, and all of a sudden he jerked the reins out of my hands. Instead of running, though, he went down on his knees, then his side. He tried to get up, but couldn't.'

'Did you hear anything?'

A blank look. 'Like what?'

'A shot? I heard one when your father was hit.'

'No.' He looked at his feet. 'I didn't hear anything but Bailey.'

'Bailey?'

'He was crying — the way horses do when they're hurt. You know?'

'Yes.' I could imagine it.

The inner door opened and a stern-faced policewoman stepped out. She wore a navy skirt and a pale blue blouse with a nametag like the officer at the reception window.

'That's for me,' Bobby said, rising.

He jogged forward, accepted some papers from the woman, and said something too low for me to overhear. Then he hurried out to the parking lot.

'Well?' Davy asked, moving over to join me. 'Learn anything?'

'Not really. He didn't even know whether Bailey had been shot. You'll probably need a necropsy.'

'Huh? A what?'

'A necropsy. Most people use the term

autopsy when they actually mean necropsy.'

'An autopsy — *necropsy* — on a *horse?*'

'Sure. Any large veterinary facility should be able to do it. Or maybe the cops will. Who knows, it might be natural causes. Wouldn't that be amusing?'

Officer Weinstein leaned out from his window. 'Detective Nuñes will see you now,' he said.

★　★　★

Nuñes turned out to be a pleasant Hispanic woman, short and compact, with straight black hair and large, almond-colored eyes. A plainclothes officer, she wore a tan skirt with matching jacket over a white cotton blouse. Rather than heels, she had brown running shoes. Absently, I noted a pale line circling the ring finger of her left hand. A wedding band had been removed recently.

'Thanks for stopping in. You look better this morning, Mr. Geller.'

I said, 'I . . . don't handle stress well.'

'You did a pretty good job yesterday.

You're quite the local hero. Channel 6 and channel 10 both ran stories on you last night.'

I blinked. 'I was on TV?'

'Six o'clock *and* eleven o'clock broadcasts.'

'Slow news day,' I muttered.

'Are you kidding? When a handicapped local man saves two people from a sniper, that's big stuff in Philly. They ran an interview with Mr. Hunt. He told how you single-handedly dragged Bobby Goldsmith and him to cover behind the dead horse, then risked your life to try to save the boy's stepfather. It doesn't get much better than that.'

I gave Davy an I'll-kill-you-later look. The last thing I wanted was to be featured on television. On two channels, yet.

'Uh . . . I don't remember much,' I said. 'It happened so fast, it's a blur.'

'Your modesty is refreshing, Mr. Geller. This way.'

Turning, she led us through a large, high-ceilinged room full of tiny desks. A few uniformed police officers sat filling out paperwork, typing at computers, or talking on phones.

She said, 'I need you to read over your statements, then sign them. That's all for today.'

Her desk sat in the far corner of the room. Davy and I slid into a pair of white plastic chairs like the ones in the waiting area. A wooden stand in the shape of a pink poodle held business cards. I picked one up: Detective F. Nuñes, Buckston Police, with address, phone number, and extension.

I put the card back, then stretched out my legs. My hands shook like palsy. I pressed my palms hard against my thighs. Tremens, hold the delirium. It would pass in a few minutes.

Nuñes picked up clipboards with statements already typed out and handed one to each of us. In sixty-five words, mine told how Mitch Goldsmith got shot. It ended with Davy dialing 911.

'There's one detail I left out,' I said. I repeated Mitch's last words.

'Tell Fifi Dows?' From her tone, I thought she recognized the name.

'Mitch was whispering. I could barely

261

hear him. I might be mistaken on the name, though. Is Fifi Dows a real person?'

'I don't know.'

I leaned forward, gauging her reactions. 'Maybe I got the name wrong. Do you know anyone else in the area named Fifi?'

'Let me do a quick Internet search.' Nuñes turned to her computer, and I watched her fingers glide across the keyboard. She read something off the monitor, typed again. I leaned to one side, but couldn't see the screen. Finally she shook her head.

'Afraid not, Mr. Geller. There's nobody named Fifi or F. Dows living in Buckston — or in any nearby town.'

I had the distinct impression she was leaving something out. She hadn't given a direct answer when I'd asked if she knew anyone named Fifi.

'You *do* know a Fifi, though,' I prodded.

An odd and somewhat hostile expression flashed across her face. Just as fast, she squelched it. I glanced at Davy. Had he noticed?

The detective snapped, 'I already looked.'

'Pit,' Davy said in a warning tone, 'don't be rude.'

'Sorry, Detective.' I leaned back, smiling an apology I didn't mean. 'I wasn't trying to offend. I haven't had my meds — I didn't think we'd be here this long.'

'Mr. Geller,' she said, voice hard, 'I *am* busy. If your statement is correct, please sign it. You too, Mr. Hunt.'

I noted that she didn't ask me to add Fifi Dows to my statement. Shrugging a little, I signed and returned the clipboard. Not my problem.

'Any news about the sniper?' Davy asked. He scrawled his signature with a John Hancock flourish.

'We're following a few leads.' Nuñes forced a smile as though happy to steer our discussion to safe ground again. Then she pushed her chair back and stood. 'Thank you for your help. If we need anything more, someone will be in touch.'

I struggled to my feet. 'Thanks.'

Davy started for the door. I took a step, then paused.

'About the horse . . . ' I said. 'Bailey's

Final Call? Was he shot, too?'

'We had a vet examine him this morning. It appears to have been natural causes. Dr. Rothman said . . . ' She rummaged around on her desk and located a yellow paper. 'Death due to heart failure. Apparently, it happens with race horses more often than people realize.'

'Thanks.' I turned toward the door, paused again. 'Is there going to be an autopsy?'

'It's routine in a murder investigation.'

'I meant on the horse.'

She shrugged. 'He wasn't shot, so it will be up to you or your insurance company.'

'Bailey's death seems like an odd coincidence to me. Would anyone here mind if Davy had one performed?'

'As the owner, that's certainly his right. I can't imagine anyone would object.' Her eyes narrowed a fraction. Was I stepping on official toes? 'I'll check with the officer in charge and let you know if there's a problem.'

'This isn't your case?'

'I'm working on it, but Captain Dobbs is lead investigator. Do you have a phone number where I can reach you?'

I gave her Davy's cell phone number.

★ ★ ★

'Are we done here?' I asked Davy in the parking lot. 'The vet said natural causes. I want to go home.'

'You win.' He shrugged. 'The police can find Mitch's killer. Who knows, maybe he was borrowing money from loan sharks and didn't pay up fast enough.'

'Maybe.' But what self-respecting loan shark would be named Fifi?

As I settled into the car seat, my brain wouldn't quit. I couldn't stop reviewing everything Nuñes had told us. And I kept coming back to her reaction when I mentioned Fifi Dows.

Her first name began with F. It couldn't be that simple . . . could it?

'What's wrong?' Davy asked.

'Give me your phone. I want to try something.'

He surrendered his cell phone. I flipped it open and, from memory, dialed the number on Nuñes' business card.

265

A male voice answered, 'Buckston Police Department.'

'Is Fifi there?' I asked.

'Hang on.'

A few clicks. Then I heard the someone pick up. 'Officer Nuñes.'

I deepened my voice an octave. 'Sorry, wrong number.' Snapping the phone shut, I told Davy what had happened.

'*Detective Nuñes* is Fifi?' he said. 'No way!'

'Probably a nickname. If the officer on duty knew, it can't be much of a secret. No wonder she didn't add it to my official statement.'

I could see him trying to connect the dots in his mind. 'How would she know Mitch Goldsmith . . . ?'

'Tell Fifi *what*? What does 'Dows' mean?'

'Got me.'

I chewed my lip. Perhaps 'Dows' hadn't been a last name. Part of another word?

Davy pulled out of Visitor's Parking. I watched the passenger-side mirror as a white Firebird trailed us onto Route 202. The driver, a stocky man with a military-style crew cut and sunglasses, did not look familiar. Nor did the empty license plate holder help — unfortunately, Pennsylvania didn't require front tags.

I said, 'I think we're being followed.'

Moving only his eyes, Davy glanced at the rear-view mirror.

'White car?' he asked.

'Yes.'

He floored the accelerator and made a sharp left turn across oncoming traffic. A truck's horn blared. I heard the squeal of brakes, but no crash followed. Davy shifted gears and sped up a twisty two-lane road, making a series of random turns. He didn't slow until we cruised down a tree-lined country lane with farms to either side.

I turned in my seat to look back. The white car had disappeared.

My memory dredged up a picture of the parking lot behind the police station. I had seen the Firebird. An employee vehicle? An unmarked police car?

'Do you think that was the killer?' Davy asked.

'Only if the killer is a cop.'

He chewed that over. 'Maybe Nuñes

put a tail on us.'

'Why? Your horse died of natural causes, as far as she's concerned.' I paused. 'Unless she lied.'

'That horse doctor — what was his name?'

'Rothman. Want me to call him?'

'Yes.' He handed over his phone again, and I dialed Information. Sure enough, the operator found a number in Doylestown for Rothman's practice and put me through.

On the second ring, a woman picked up and said: 'Rothman Veterinary.'

I thumbed on the speakerphone so Davy could hear.

'Hi,' I said. 'I'm calling about Bailey's Final Call. The police said Dr. Rothman examined him?'

'Uh . . . who is this? If you're another reporter . . . '

'No, ma'am. My name is Peter Geller. I — '

'Oh, I saw you on the news last night.' Her manner softened noticeably. 'Hold on, Mr. Geller. Dr. Rothman will be free in a moment.'

Classical music began to play, tinny

and small through the speaker. Davy pulled off onto a broad gravel shoulder and put the engine in neutral.

'Detective Fifi told the truth,' he said.

'We'll see.'

He opened his mouth, but the music cut off and a man announced, 'This is Dr. Rothman. How may I help you?'

I identified myself. 'David Hunt is with me,' I said. 'We're looking for closure about Bailey, and the police said you examined him last night?'

'That's right.'

'Any idea what happened?'

He cleared his throat. 'As far as I can tell, he died of heart failure. As for the cause . . . ' I envisioned him shrugging on the other end of the line. 'It could have been a previously undetected heart flaw. A virus. Or something else entirely.'

'He wasn't shot?'

'There were no bullet wounds.'

'What about puncture marks? Could he have been doped with something?'

Rothman gave a humorless bark of a laugh. 'A race horse is a walking pincushion. Between drawing blood, Lasix shots, inoculations, and vitamins, they get more needles than you can count. If someone doped him, you'd never notice one more hole. And half the drugs used today leave no traces behind, anyway. Could he have been drugged? Sure. Do I think he was? I doubt it.'

'Did you take a blood sample? Davy wants blood work run.'

'Already sent to the lab. I won't see results until tomorrow, though.'

'So there's no *official* cause of death yet?'

'No-o-o.' He drawled it out. 'But, like I said, I'm sure it will come down to heart failure. I can let you know when I get the report, if that helps.'

'Thanks.' I gave him Davy's fax and cell phone numbers. 'Please call any time with news. Mr. Hunt would like a copy of the lab results. You can bill him for it.'

'Anything more?'

What else might prove helpful?

'Did you order a specific set of tests?' I asked.

'All the standard ones.'

'Are there any others you can get

— never mind the expense — that might catch something you'd normally miss?'

He paused. 'Is there something I ought to know about Bailey's death?'

'No. At least, nothing specific. Call it a hunch. Mr. Hunt has a feeling something isn't quite right. Having Bailey and Mitch Goldsmith die together is, well, an odd coincidence. Too odd.'

'There are a few more tests . . . but they'll add a week to the results. And they aren't cheap.'

'Run them.'

'Mr. Hunt will pay the bill?'

I glanced at Davy, who nodded.

'Yes,' I said. 'Charge it to David Hunt's credit card.' I gave him Davy's AmEx number from memory. 'Don't worry about costs. And if it can be expedited in any way — '

'I understand. I'll take care of it. Anything else I can help you with?'

'Do you know Mitch's friend, Fifi?'

'Afraid not. I wasn't their vet. You might ask Dr. Christiansen. His practice is in Plumstead, the next town over. Great guy.'

'Thanks.'

'Call if you need anything else.' He hung up.

I returned Davy's phone. He drummed his fingers on the steering wheel, gaze distant.

'It *is* too much of a coincidence,' he said. 'Bailey was doped. I know it.'

'Let's see what the lab says.'

'What's our next step?'

'I need to eat. Low blood sugar is starting to bother me.' I hoped it was low blood sugar.

'Want a beer with your pizza?' he asked.

It was a test, and I knew it. Would I give in to alcohol or stick it out till the end?

'Juice,' I said. Pain I could live with. Shakes I could suffer in silence. I still had the bottle of aspirin in my pocket; it would have to do.

Davy smiled. 'After lunch, what next?'

'Back to the scene of the crime. I want to look around the farm.'

★　★　★

Davy's satellite navigation system steered us into the center of Doylestown. A shop-lined main street led us past the county courthouse. There weren't many restaurants to choose from, but we finally settled on a Greek diner in a strip mall. Chicken souvlaki, orange juice, and French fries took the edge off my hunger and calmed my shaking hands. The waitress gave us directions back to 202, so Davy over-tipped her by ten dollars.

Twenty minutes later, we turned into Black Fox Farm, passed between the stone gateposts, and cruised up the long driveway. Today the place had a curiously deserted look, like a movie set after the actors had all gone home: no people, no horses, no signs of life anywhere. The battered horse-van still sat by the exercise ring. The only other vehicles were the red convertible, now parked directly in front of the house, and a metallic purple motorcycle next to it.

Davy pulled up behind 'Horse Kid' and climbed out. My legs felt like water, but I got them working.

Davy marched to the porch. I followed. They didn't have a doorbell, so he rapped hard on the frame. Nobody answered. We exchanged a glance.

'Try the barn,' I said. 'Bobby's probably taking care of the livestock.'

'Want to wait in the car?'

'No.' I tried the front door. The knob turned easily, so I pushed it open an inch. 'I want to poke around inside.'

'You can't. That's breaking and entering!'

'What breaking? Besides, I have to sit down in a comfy chair for a few minutes and rest. Didn't Mitch say I was welcome any time?'

'Pit . . . '

'Keep the kid busy for fifteen minutes. There's something I want to check out.'

Davy set off with an I-don't-like-this-idea expression. I grinned. By now he ought to understand the value of risk. Besides, wasn't I a local hero? Missy wouldn't press charges.

I pushed inside, flipped the light switch, and looked around.

A tall-backed oak chair studded with coat hooks stood against the right wall, flanked by tasteful steel engravings of horsing scenes. A white ceramic umbrellastand stuffed with umbrellas sat to the left. Through the doorway straight ahead, I spotted a kitchen with 1960s-era fixtures.

A distant banging noise, over and over, came from somewhere upstairs. The breath caught in my throat. Someone was in the house. A burglar?

I crept forward, through the kitchen with its worn linoleum floor and floral wallpaper, to a tiny butler's staircase in the rear. The banging grew steadily louder. I heard faint music now, too. I put my foot on the bottom step and paused, listening.

Music . . . banging . . . and faint animal grunts.

I could have slapped myself. Good thing I hadn't called Davy or the police. It had been a long time, but I still recognized the sounds of vigourous sex. Someone was having a good time up there. Missy? With her husband not even in the grave? No — she was in the hospital.

Or Bobby? That made more sense. The 'horse kid' car out front pointed to him. And the purple motorcycle probably meant a friend. From the sounds of things, they would be busy for a while.

Chuckling, I wandered through the ground floor, keeping to the throw rugs, trying to move silently. The living room had plastic-sheathed furniture, a dozen pink roses in a vase, and more tasteful horse pictures. Then, off the dining room, I found what I had been searching for: Mitch's office.

It was small and cluttered, much as I'd imagined, with a battered steel desk, a wooden filing cabinet topped with a fax machine, a small pink couch that must have been one of Missy's cast-offs . . . and stacked against the wall, four large shipping cartons.

Those interested me. The top one had been opened; its flaps stuck up. I peeked inside at sealed plastic containers: iPods — and not cheap models, either. One had been removed from the carton. I remembered Bobby's from the police station. The kid must have swiped it from this stash.

Stepping back, I estimated forty iPods per carton, a hundred and sixty total.

What would Mitch be doing with so many?

I turned to the desk, plopped onto its old-fashioned wooden chair, then rolled forward on squeaky wheels. Maybe I could find the answer here.

A pocket-sized address book lay at hand, so I flipped to 'F' — but only found three entries. No Fifi. I flipped back to 'D' — no Dows. Could I have misunderstood? What sounded like Dows? Tows? I tried 'T.' Nothing.

I snapped the address book shut and slipped it into my pocket; I'd go through it at my leisure, then get it back to Missy somehow.

What about the cubbyholes? A large three-up check ledger had been tucked into one, so I pulled it out and paged to the last stub, $3,554.00 for feed.

I worked backwards. Mitch had been diligent about recording not only checks, but deposits. I could see at a glance where all his money had come from and gone. As I'd suspected, the farm barely scraped by. If not for a single big deposit from two days ago, Mitch would have been overdrawn by nearly forty thousand dollars.

Besides the usual utility and feed bills — could hay and oats cost that much? — I found a few deposit entries of interest:

BFC (1st) . . . $75,000 R (rent) $2,500

BFC had to be Bailey's Final Call — probably Davy's down-payment on the horse. Every penny had gone out the next day to pay what must have been long overdue bills.

Who or what was 'R'? I flipped back through the stubs looking at deposit records. Sure enough, R paid his rent like clockwork on the fifteenth of every month. But what was being rented for so much money?

There were no entries for Fifi Dows, nor any combination of her initials.

I had just started looking for Mitch's insurance policy when a floorboard squeaked behind me. I swiveled in my chair.

'What are you doing?' Bobby demanded from the doorway. He wore nothing but boxer shorts done in red, white, and blue like the American flag, and to my surprise, he had not an ounce of fat on his body, from six-pack abs to sharply defined shoulders and biceps. More than anything, he looked like a Calvin Kline underwear model.

'Hi, Bobby. We knocked a bunch of times. Since the door was open, I didn't think your mother would mind if I waited inside.' I grasped my cane. If he wanted to beat me to a pulp, I might not be able to stop him — but I'd try.

'Well, *I* mind.' With two quick steps, he closed the distance between us. He loomed over me, fists tight, the mingled odors of sweat and sex rolling off his body. 'Where is Mr. Hunt?'

'Out looking for you.'

He stretched out his hand, and I half cringed. But instead of grabbing me, he reached past and slapped the desk shut.

'Keep out of our stuff!'

'I need the phone number for your vet — '

'Dr. Christiansen?' He hesitated. 'What for?'

'Davy wants an autopsy performed on Bailey.'

His fists unclenched. 'You're too late. Valley Protein picked him up this morning.'

'Who?'

'Valley Protein — the disposal company.'

'What! Who gave them permission?'

'I did. *After* I checked with the police.'

I blinked. 'You mean Detective Nuñes?'

'Yes.'

The breath caught in my throat. Nuñes had told us that we could order an autopsy. But if she'd already given permission for the horse to be disposed of . . .

Maybe I had the timeline wrong.

I said, 'When did you talk to her about it? This morning?'

'Yeah. At the police station.'

So much for that idea. She had to be covering something up, just like she'd held out on her name. She had pushed the 'accidental death' theory a little too hard for my satisfaction.

Bobby went on, 'It's summer — you can't leave a dead horse lying around. Bailey was already attracting turkey vultures. Oh! Hang on.' He darted from the room, then returned a moment later with a folded-up piece of paper, which he handed to me.

It was a bill for two hundred and fifty dollars, a disposal fee to remove Bailey's Final Call. It had the company name and phone number. Davy would have to call and stop them from doing whatever they did with dead horses. Dog food?

'Since Bailey is yours,' Bobby said, arms folded, 'I think *you* should pay for it. I paid them cash this afternoon.'

'Of course.' I forced another smile. 'I'll give it to Davy. He'll take care of it. I think he has his checkbook.' Rising, I stuck the bill in my pocket, then limped toward the door. There I paused. 'Why so many iPods?'

'We sell them on eBay.'

'Ah.' Perhaps a side business begun to keep food on the table in leaner times. It might even be more successful than horse farming, aside from flukes like Bailey.

'Want a deal?' He pulled one from the open box — a white iPod with a large video screen, sealed in heavy plastic. 'A hundred and twenty — that's better than wholesale.'

'I don't listen to music — '

He frowned and thrust it into my hands

anyway. The room see-sawed. I gazed past Bobby at the door. I had to get out.

'It's more than music,' he said, pushing closer. He jabbed at the package with one finger. I jumped. 'See here? It plays audio-books, podcasts, TV shows, and movies. Everything you need is inside. It's a sweet deal. You should take it.'

His voice sounded impossibly far away now, as though at the end of a long tunnel. My vision began to dim at the corners of my eyes, narrowing in on just his face.

Another panic attack was coming. I had to get out of here.

'Well?' he demanded.

Gulping hard, I nodded. *Buy the damn thing.* He'd back off. I could get away.

'Credit? Card?' I tried to sound normal.

'I gotta charge you an extra two percent.'

'Uh-huh.'

I fumbled for my wallet. My hands shook so much, I dropped everything. Credit cards, organ donor card, and driver's license spilled across the floor.

'I'll get it,' he said, bending and scooping everything back into place except my Visa card. 'This one?'

'Uh . . . huh . . . '

He found an old-fashioned charge machine in a desk drawer, loaded a credit slip, and ran my card through. As he filled out the total with a stub of a pencil, my eyes kept drifting toward the doorway. I could make a break for it —

Bobby grinned, suddenly *too close*, almost in my face. 'You'll love it. Trust me. I just need an email address . . . '

Babbling something incoherent, I hugged the iPod and hurried through the doorway. I'd be all right once I got outside. Down the hall, through the kitchen. My legs tried to buckle. I struggled to lock my knees.

Floorboards squeaked behind me. *Keep moving.* The hair on the back of my neck prickled. *Don't look.* Another step. A trickle of sweat ran down my left side, leaving a cold trail. Another step. I could hear Bobby breathing.

In a sudden rush, I shouldered the front door open and burst onto the porch. *Free.* I clutched the railing, gasping, eyes wide.

The world stopped closing in. The earth stopped rolling. My chest grew lighter and I could breathe.

'Are you okay?' Bobby asked, still behind me. 'Mr. Geller?'

'I'll — I'll be all right . . . Give a minute . . . '

Where had Davy gotten off to? I couldn't see him anywhere. I had to distract the kid before he went looking.

My attention focused on the front steps. A little accident should do it.

I worked my way over to the top step, hanging onto the railing with my right hand, and started down to the yard. On the second step, I let my knees buckle. With a yelp of fear, I dropped my cane and the iPod and pitched forward. My grip on the railing kept me from tumbling to the ground, so I hung half suspended in air. I could either be saved or — if necessary — save myself, depending on what Bobby did. What *would* he do?

Teetering, I gave a very authentic moan.

Bare feet pounded on the porch. A second later, a hand grabbed my shoulder and hauled me back. *Saved.* Good kid, all right. My first impression hadn't been wrong.

'Did you hurt yourself?' Bobby said.

'I . . . don't think so. Not much.' How far could I play up my 'accident' without him getting suspicious? 'I thought I was going to break my neck!'

'Good thing I was here.'

I searched his face. Concern, maybe a hint of pity. Best he should view me as a harmless old cripple.

Looping my arm across his neck and shoulder, he helped me down the steps, then went back for my cane. I leaned on it harder than I needed to. Then he retrieved my iPod.

'It's not broken or anything,' he said, brushing off the plastic packaging. 'Here you go.'

'Thanks.'

'Can I get you anything? A glass of water, maybe?'

'No . . . just let me rest for a minute.' I wiped at my face. God, I was soaked with sweat.

'Want to come back inside?'

'I . . . I don't think I can make it up the steps.'

He looked relieved. Instead, I nodded at the lawn chairs Mitch had placed under the huge oak. Nobody had put them away.

'Help me over there?'

'Sure.'

He steadied my arm as I hobbled across and sat hard. My hands still trembled. I exaggerated it to good effect. No sign of Davy yet.

'You better get dressed,' I told him. 'Your mother would have a fit if she saw you outside like that.'

'Yeah.' Without another word, he turned and ran back to the house. The front door banged. I imagined him throwing the deadbolts.

Davy was just returning from the barns. Perfect timing.

'Find anything?' I asked.

'Nah. The barn by the house has a bunch of horses inside. That old guy, Carl, was cleaning out the stalls.'

'What old guy?'

'You saw him — he was at the exercise

ring with Mitch when we got here yesterday.'

'Thin, fifty-five or so, bib overalls and a Phillies baseball cap?'

'That's Carl. I asked him about the murder. He said he was giving a riding lesson and didn't hear anything. He didn't know anything had happened till the police and ambulance showed up.'

'I'm not surprised. I think we can safely cross him off as a suspect. The little girl, too. What about the other barn?'

'It's padlocked, so I couldn't get inside to check it out. How about you? Have any luck?'

'Yep.' I grinned and patted my pocket. 'I swiped Mitch's address book. Unfortunately, the kid surprised me rifling through the office desk. I thought he was going to punch me out, so I made a strategic withdrawal.'

'Ran away, you mean.'

'Something like that.' I glanced at the house and noted a shadow at one of the dining room windows. That had to be Bobby. A second shadow drifted over to him — the girlfriend, no doubt.

Wouldn't it be amusing if his girlfriend turned out to be Detective Fifi? Her wedding ring *had* been recently removed. And with Bobby's tight little body, who could blame her for a little cradle-robbing?

'Well, what did you expect?' Davy chuckled. 'I would have punched you out in his position. How come he didn't answer when I knocked?'

'He didn't hear you. He had a girl upstairs, and they were going at it hammer and tongs.'

'So we've hit another dead end.'

'Don't forget I have the address book. And I've got a couple of presents for you.' I fished out the Valley Protein bill. 'The kid had Bailey picked up this morning. You'd better call the removal company and save Bailey from the dog food factory. You might still want an autopsy, depending on the blood results. I bet they have a freezer where they can store him for you. Of course, it'll cost a bit . . . '

He pulled out his phone and began to dial. 'What next? Are we done here?'

'Not quite.' I handed him the iPod. 'Happy birthday.'

'Uh. Thanks. But it's not my birthday yet.'

'Four months, two days early. Close enough.' Rising, I started for the path around the house. 'I want to see the scene of the crime again.'

★　★　★

Davy talked Valley Protein into putting Bailey's Final Call on ice pending the insurance company's investigation. Apparently it wasn't that odd or unusual of a request. Fifty bucks a day took care of everything.

Bailey might have been carted off, but even without my trick memory, I would have known the spot where he had lain from the flattened grass. A small, rust-colored stain marked where Mitch had fallen.

Closing my eyes, I replayed yesterday's murder.

Bailey on the ground. Bobby across the horse's neck. Mitch facing us as blood colored the silver letters of his shirt . . . I crossed to Mitch's last standing position and turned around.

With Bailey in front of me, the first barn to my right, the second barn directly behind me, and Davy slightly to my left . . . a bullet from the woods would have hit me in my side.

But Mitch had been shot in the back.

I turned and stared at Barn No. 2, with its dark red paint, the hex sign under the eaves, and the peeling white trim. It had no windows, but this close I noticed gaps between side boards. And the second-story hayloft had doors, one of which sat open a foot. A sniper could have shot Mitch from up there. Maybe even from the roof.

In my mind, I replayed the loud *crack* of the shot, but couldn't tell where it had originated. Even the slight echo as the sound bounced back from the main house offered no significant help.

Turning, I faced the woods. Yellow crime-scene tape flapped in the faint breeze.

'What's all that?' I pointed with my cane.

'The cops found a rifle shell over there.

The sniper lay in the grass to take his shot.'

'When did they find it? Yesterday?'

'Yeah. They had twenty people combing the area. Why?'

'Someone planted that shell. The shot came from the barn.'

'You're sure?'

'Do you need to ask?'

He shrugged. 'Okay. Now what? Back to Detective Fifi? The police should be told — '

I snorted. 'For all we know, *she* was the sniper. What better way of escaping? She could just blend in with the police going over the farm.'

He gaped. 'You don't really think — '

'No, I'm just babbling. But nothing would surprise me these days.'

'So what's our next move?'

'I want to go shopping. I want a real shirt with buttons.' As I said it, I studied the second barn. Davy hadn't gotten a peek inside. But now I wanted to see its contents. 'After dark, we'll come back with a bolt cutter. *That* will be breaking and entering.'

'Pit . . . ' He shook his head.

'No one will press charges if we're caught.'

'When we're caught, you mean.'

Movement from the house caught my eye. Bobby, still in his patriotic boxers, had stepped onto the small back porch. He leaned on the railing and stared at us.

'We've got an audience,' I muttered. 'Quick, act natural.'

Davy glanced over his shoulder and waved. Bobby gave a curt nod, turned, and stalked back inside. A not-so-subtle hint for us to get out.

Then, from the front of the house, I heard the roar of a motorcycle engine. Bobby's girlfriend?

'Let's get out of here,' I said, starting for the front yard.

When we reached the BMW, the purple bike was gone. Somehow, I couldn't picture Detective Fifi on it.

⋆　⋆　⋆

We spent the rest of the afternoon running errands. Doylestown didn't have a hardware store, or we couldn't find it, so K-Mart supplied two small but powerful flashlights and a bolt cutter. Davy thought it would nip off the padlock with little difficulty.

Muttering, 'Now for a shirt,' I started for the clothing department.

'Are you out of your mind?' Davy caught my arm.

'Forget designer labels.' He had been fussy about his appearance in college, and dating a model had only made things worse. 'Clothes are clothes. Get 'em while we're here.'

'Bad enough I'm wearing a grocery-store tee-shirt. No way am I buying the rest of my wardrobe *here*.'

I shrugged. 'It's your money.'

'Damn right!'

★ ★ ★

We paid for the tools and left. To the annoyance of drivers behind us, Davy stuck to the speed limit on Route 202. That probably attracted more notice than speeding would have. Not that I could point it out.

As we neared the outlet stores and whatever garments Davy considered suitable for an evening of crime, I watched the road. Twice police cars cruised past in the opposite direction. Neither slowed to check us out.

Fifteen minutes later, we came to our Best Western. Davy kept going, and soon a couple of strip malls appeared. I took in the signs. Orvis . . . Bose . . . Mikasa . . . Davy would be in his element here.

We parked in front of an Urban Safari. After my usual moans and groans from being cramped up, which Davy ignored, I followed him in.

The place had a weird retro-safari vibe going. Images of lions and giraffes superimposed over skyscrapers, while yuppies and dinks fished from the roofs of Audis. Yep, Davy's sort of place.

Skirting high-tech silver mannequins, I made a beeline for the clearance rack. Sometimes it pays to be small and thin. Sure enough, I found a bunch of mark-downs in my size. Soft fabrics and earthy colors suited me, so I picked out three presentable shirts in various shades of brown and two pairs of brown pants. I left them at the checkout counter with a bubblegum-chewing girl who couldn't have been more than sixteen, then wandered over to check on Davy. He could pay for everything and haul it out to the car.

'What would Cree say?' I asked. He was holding up olive green shorts covered with what must have been two dozen pockets with heavy steel zippers. 'Are pockets 'in' this year?'

'I do fashion fine by myself.' He put the zipper-pants back quickly, though. 'What about you? Find any clothes you want?'

'Lots. My stuff's waiting at checkout. I'm done.'

'But you haven't tried anything on!'

'Everything will fit.'

He shook his head, turned to the rack, and pulled out a pair identical to the last, only dusty blue. Then he put those back and pulled out burnt-orange shorts with coils of chains hanging from every seam . . . a Goth nightmare. Did he intend to go through every garment? Better him than me.

I said, 'I'll be sitting out front. Call me if you need me.'

'Okay.'

I pushed through the door and into the heat again. The sun had moved enough to put the bench in shadow. The deep warmth of the wood felt soothing against my back.

Settling down as comfortably as I could, I flipped open Mitch's black address book. It contained little more than names and phone numbers, beginning with 'Abramson, Eli and Faye' and ending with 'Zensen, Jon.' I started from the beginning.

No patterns emerged, though I learned the names and addresses of their priest, their church choir director, and dozens of friends and relatives. As an added bonus, it had all the companies with which Mitch did business: feed stores, hardware companies, race tracks, horse trailer rentals, that sort of thing. He even knew a blacksmith.

Then I stopped cold. Fifi Nuñes' name almost leaped off the page. Mitch had listed her under 'P' — for 'Police.' And he had two numbers for her, the office number and a cell phone number.

I could have slapped myself for not checking under 'P' first. Her listing came before 'Det. Arthur Dawson.' She had extension 127, and Dawson had 128. Adjoining desks? *Partners?*

'Tell Fifi Dows' could have meant, 'Tell Fifi and Dawson.' Mitch had barely been able to speak. Or maybe 'Daws' rather than 'Dows' . . . 'Daws' could have been a nickname.

But tell them what? That he'd been shot? Or something more?

I looked up, gaze unfocused, trying to think it through logically. Mitch . . . Bobby . . . Missy . . . too much didn't make sense yet.

A motorcycle roared down the highway right in front of me. A *metallic purple* motorcycle.

My attention snapped to it. I scrabbled to my feet.

It was the same one I'd seen next to Bobby's convertible. I would have sworn to it. And the rider wasn't a girl, it was a young man — very thin, like Bobby, almost elfin. His unbuttoned shirt hung open and flapping in the breeze, leaving his bare chest exposed.

There was no mistaking his sex.

I sat. No wonder Bobby had reacted so violently when he found me in the house. I'd almost 'outed' him. His reaction made a lot more sense now. And so much for Detective Fifi being his girlfriend . . .

I peeked in the Urban Safari's window. Davy browsed past, a blood red shirt in one hand, but nothing else yet. He had such an intense expression, I almost laughed. If little old ladies got in his way, he'd mow them down.

Returning to my seat, I finished reading through the address book. No more Fifis. No Dows. It came back to the two detectives.

Maybe Mitch knew them socially . . . through church? Or the Elks Club, or the Rotarians? No — he'd put them under 'Police.' All his social contacts went in under their last names.

Returning to the 'P' section, I studied the entries. Every other 'P' name had been alphabetized, from Sara Paul to Tom

Purdom, as though copied from a previous address book. Fifi Nuñes and Arthur Dawson came last . . . added more recently than all the others.

★ ★ ★

Half an hour later, heading back to the Best Western, I filled Davy in on the purple motorcycle.

'Huh,' was all he said.

Then I told him what I'd discovered in Mitch's book. He pursed his lips and nodded.

'Detective Fifi knows a lot more than she's saying,' he added. 'She's been lying to us all along.'

'Not technically. She doesn't *know* any Fifis. She *is* a Fifi. And there probably *aren't* any others in the area.'

'Lying by omission is still lying.'

'Kinda.' I yawned. 'What time is it?'

He glanced at his watch. 'Almost six.'

'It should be dark enough by eleven to hit the farm. Assuming they keep early hours . . . '

'How about dinner?'

'Maybe a nap first, then dinner. I'm exhausted.'

The Best Western appeared. Davy turned into the parking lot and circled to the left.

I sat up straight. Parked directly in front of our door sat the white Mustang that had followed us from the Buckston police station. The driver with the crew cut and the sunglasses leaned against the passenger side, arms folded, face expressionless. He stood as we neared.

'Want to bet he's Fifi's partner?' I whispered.

'No.' Davy pulled into the space on the other side of the Mustang. He didn't cut the engine.

Sunglasses-man stalked around the car.

'David Hunt?' he asked. He pulled a badge from his pocket and held it up. 'Buckston Police.'

'Detective Dawson?' Davy countered.

'Yes.' Dawson reached past Davy, turned the key in the BMW's ignition, and pulled it out. He dropped it into his breast pocket. Then, in an emotionless voice, he said, 'May I see your operator's license and vehicle registration, sir.' It was not a question.

Davy blanched but pulled out his driver's license. The convertible's registration was in the glove compartment. I retrieved it.

Dawson took everything to his Mustang, climbed inside, and spoke into a radio handset. Slowly, Davy sank in his seat as though trying to disappear.

'Don't worry,' I said. 'It's not like this car is stolen.'

Davy didn't answer.

' . . . Is it?'

'Oh, shut up!'

When the detective came back, he held a small clipboard. The kind that held traffic tickets.

'Mr. Hunt,' he said, 'were you aware of an oncoming truck when you made a turn across traffic on Route 202 this morning?'

'Yes,' Davy said. 'I didn't know who you were, and — '

The detective cut him off. 'I am issuing a citation for reckless driving. You endangered the lives of other motorists. I suggest you take more care on our roads in the future. Sign here.'

'Can't you let us off with a warning, officer?' I asked.

'Not this time.'

'Where do you want me to sign?' Davy asked.

Dawson jabbed a finger at the bottom of the clipboard. Without another peep, Davy scrawled his name. Dawson tore off the ticket and handed it over, along with Davy's keys.

I wouldn't have thought it possible, but Davy sank even lower in his seat.

'Excuse me,' I said.

'What?'

'Are you Fifi Nuñes's partner?'

'We sometimes work together. It depends on the case.'

'On Mitch Goldsmith's case?'

'We are both assisting Captain Dobbs with that investigation, yes.'

'No, Mitch's other case.'

He hesitated, studying me. I wished I could have seen his eyes.

'I cannot discuss ongoing investigations,' he said.

Interesting. Something had come up

with Mitch and the police before the sniper. What?

'I understand — and I'm not trying to interfere.' I paused. 'It's just that before he died, Mitch Goldsmith gave me this message . . . '

'What message?'

'He said, 'Tell Fifi and Daws,' mumbled a few words I couldn't quite understand, and passed out.' Partly a lie, but it ought to catch Dawson's interest. 'He called you Daws?'

'My friends do.'

So Dawson considered Mitch a friend. Interesting.

'Do you have any news about Missy? Is she still in the hospital?'

'She should be home now. Mitch's viewing is at ten o'clock tomorrow morning at the Himmelbach Funeral Home.'

Davy asked, 'That's in Buckston?'

'On Route 202. You won't have trouble finding it.'

'Thanks.'

Dawson stepped back. 'Drive safely, sir.'

* * *

It was closer to 11:30 that night when we reached Black Fox Farm. Davy cut the headlights as he pulled into the driveway, coasting through the poplars and birches then onto the grass. Crickets burred in the grass, and something small to our left made a rustling sound in the bushes. A raccoon? Maybe the eponymous fox?

'I can go alone, if you want,' Davy said.

'Not a chance.'

'I was hoping you'd say that.'

I twisted in my seat, but couldn't see Route 202. We'd be safe from Fifi or Daws if they happened past. Anyone leaving the house would spot us at once, of course, but it was late enough that everyone should be in for the night.

Davy passed me a flashlight. I didn't turn it on; my eyes were growing used to the dark. With the moon up and a faint glow shining in from streetlights on the highway, I could get to the barn.

Davy climbed out, and I did the same. The clicks of our doors shutting sounded like gunshots in the night. As we walked up the driveway, feet crunching softly on the gravel, I spotted two dim lights in the farmhouse windows, one on the second floor — probably a bedroom — and one deep in the ground floor. The kitchen? A yellow bug light cast a dim glow across the front porch.

Like a cat, Davy padded down the path between house and stables, making no sounds at all. I clunked along after him. Between my shuffling walk, gasps for breath, and occasional loud tap as my cane struck something hard, I felt like the world's most incompetent burglar.

At last, panting, I caught up with Davy at the second barn. He pulled out the bolt cutter.

'Light?' he said.

I thumbed on my flashlight and aimed it at the door. I found a handle and two metal brackets for a padlock, but the lock itself was gone. We exchanged a glance.

'We should come back in an hour,' I whispered. 'Might be someone inside.'

'Shh!' He pressed his ear to the door. I strained to listen. *Nothing*.

'Risk versus reward,' he muttered. 'Isn't

that what you keep saying?'

He pulled the door open a foot, hinges squealing, and a band of yellow light caught me. It wasn't all that bright, but after the darkness, it seemed piercing.

Blinking and shading my eyes, I retreated a few steps. If bullets came flying, I didn't want to catch one.

Davy darted inside. I counted to ten. Then ten more. Finally Davy stuck his head out.

'No one here. Come on.'

I followed him inside, and he pulled the door shut behind us. A bare yellow bulb — maybe sixty watts — dangled from a cord overhead. The hard-packed dirt floor had been swept clean, and the walls had been painted white in the not too distant past. Stalls to the left held storage — boxes of all sizes, a stack of rusting bicycles and bicycle parts, wooden pallets. In the center of the room stood a huge riding lawnmower with still-green clippings on its blades. To the right sat a dusty workbench covered with ancient computers, hard drives, cases, and parts.

Nothing terribly incriminating — about

what you'd expect to find in a barn these days. Then I noticed a ladder leading up to the hay loft. Was that where the shooter had been hiding?

I nudged Davy and pointed.

'Take a look upstairs. Maybe the rifle's there.'

'Okay.' He set down his tools, went to the ladder, and climbed out of sight.

I wandered around the lawnmower and came to the rear wall. It took a moment, but I realized it wasn't the back of the building. A section of the barn had been fixed up professionally, and two steel security doors, the kind you'd normally find on the outside of a house, faced in at me.

Both doors had peepholes, so I peeped into the first. Even backwards, I knew peepholes worked, distorting images smaller instead of larger. I saw only blackness, though — no light source inside.

I tried the knob, and it turned. *Risk versus reward.* Taking a deep breath, I pushed into a dark room, switched on my flash-light, and swept its beam across an unmade twin-sized bed, a night table with a 1950s-era lamp, a battered oak dresser with a round Art Deco mirror, and a bookcase holding ribbons and trophies. Posters on the walls showed horses. Bobby's bedroom?

I pulled the door shut, then crossed to the bookcase. Aside from a couple of small soccer cups, the trophies were all horse-related. Dates ran back twelve years. The kid must have been born in the saddle.

Next I moved to the dresser. A half dozen pictures in cheap frames showed Bobby with various horses in the winner's circle, often with his mother and another man I didn't recognize. No pictures of Mitch . . . but then Mitch was his stepfather.

What did Bobby read for pleasure? I poked through a pile of magazines on the floor by the bed. *Blood Sport, Equestrian Times,* and *Fast Ride* mingled with tech magazines like *Alt.2600, Email Today,* and *Wired.*

No real surprises. I returned to the barn's main room and eased the door shut. When I turned, I saw the second steel door now standing ajar. Seeping around the edges came the bright, flickering glow of a television.

Cold prickled at the back of my neck. Bobby must have been inside. Had he seen Davy? Had he seen *me*? He'd almost struck me in the house. What would he do if he caught me here?

'Don't move!'

Something hard jabbed the center of my back. I stiffened.

'Bobby?'

'Mr. Geller?'

I shuffled around, leaning hard on my cane, trying to look as old and feeble and helpless as possible. It had worked in the house . . . even if it cost me the price of an iPod.

Bobby still wore those red, white, and blue boxers, but with a gray U.S. Air Force tee-shirt and flip-flops. And he held a rusted pitchfork leveled at my back. He had poked me with one of the prongs.

'Are you crazy? Put that thing down!' I said as loud as I could, trying for a parental Voice of Authority. It came out more as a Squeak of Discomfort.

'Shut up!' Bobby snapped. 'I'm sick of

you spying on me!'

The wild look in his eyes alarmed me more than anything else. If he thought I was spying, what would he do if he found Davy upstairs?

I had to buy more time.

'There's been another shooting,' I blurted out. It was the first thing that popped into my head.

'Shut up!'

Then a voice from beyond the lawn-mower broke in: 'Pit! Where are you?'

It was Davy. He stood in the doorway, peering at us like he'd just arrived. He must have heard my warning. But how had he gotten outside? The loft doors had to be fifteen feet above the ground.

'Over here!' I waved and started in his direction as fast as I could. Bobby hesitated.

'Wait!' the kid finally cried. He lowered the pitchfork and ran to catch up. 'Who did you say was shot?'

Too late. He'd told me more with his answer than he'd intended.

'No one was shot,' I said. 'You scared me with the pitchfork. It was the first thing I thought of.'

'Oh.' He actually looked relieved.

I joined Davy. 'I found him,' I said. 'He was here, just like his mother said he would be.'

'Did you ask him your question?' Davy said.

I blinked. Question?

'What question?' Bobby said, staring at me.

Think fast. 'About Detective Nuñes,' I said. 'She told us yesterday morning, after you left, that Davy could get an autopsy done on Bailey. But you said she gave you permission to dispose of him before we got there. It's been bothering me.'

'Maybe it was my second trip to the police station, not the first. I wasn't paying attention.'

'Second trip?'

'Yeah. I brought papers to my mother at the hospital. She signed her statement for Detective Nuñes, then I dropped it off. That was right after lunch. She must have given me permission then.'

'Oh,' I said. 'That explains it.'

Davy said, 'Come on. Let's get to the motel.'

We left Bobby standing in the doorway, still holding his pitchfork.

*   *   *

My mouth went dry and I shook all over when we reached the BMW. I could have used a drink — beer, whiskey, anything alcoholic.

Davy put the car in gear, made a U-turn, and pulled out fast. He flipped on the headlights when we hit the highway.

'Thanks for the warning,' he said. 'I was about to climb down when I heard you talking to Bobby.'

'How did you get outside?'

'There's a big nail below the loft doors. I hooked my belt onto it and eased myself down. That only left a five-foot drop. Of course, I couldn't get my belt back — I left it hanging there . . . '

'We'll get it tomorrow.'

'So, aren't you going to ask me what I found?'

I looked at him. 'You found something?'

'Take a look at this!' He reached into his shirt pocket and pulled out a shell casing with a handkerchief. It was about three quarters of an inch long and shiny brass.

'Where was it?'

'In the corner, where the ceiling slopes down almost to the floor. You wouldn't see it normally, but my flashlight picked it out.'

'Good job.' It confirmed my theory about the shooter being in the second barn. 'I don't suppose you saw a rifle?'

'No sign of one.'

It had been a lot to hope for.

'What next?' Davy said.

'We speak to Detective Fifi again. First thing in the morning. Then we'll have to attend Mitch's viewing at the funeral parlor . . . '

'You know who did it, don't you?'

I shrugged. 'My list of suspects is narrowing.'

'Dawson?' Davy probably had visions of his reckless driving ticket being thrown out by a sympathetic judge.

'I think it was Bobby.'

'No way!' he said. 'He was with us

when it happened. And he's just a kid.'

'He may not have pulled the trigger, but I know he's involved. As for being a kid . . . ' I remembered the trophies in his bedroom. The dates had gone back twelve years. If he'd started riding competitively at age ten . . . how old would that make him? 'He's in his twenties. Maybe his mid-twenties.'

'No way!' he said again.

'You're only saying that because he's small. But think about it. Jockeys are *always* small. Give him a youthful face, and I can see how he'd pass for a teenager. Especially when he wants to.' As he'd clearly done for our benefit. And probably for the police's.

'But *why*?'

'I don't know — yet. And the hard part will be proving it. He covered everything pretty well.'

★   ★   ★

We returned to the Best Western and spent an uneventful night. As usual, Davy was up with the sun the next morning, showering and bustling around our room. Even with the pillow over my head, I could hear his damn cheerful whistling.

'Will you cut that out?' I snarled.

He laughed. 'Want a Dr. Pepper? You need some caffeine.'

I mumbled obscenities into the mattress. But finally I roused myself enough to sit up.

An hour later, after a truly wretched breakfast of burnt toast, bitter coffee, and runny scrambled eggs at a nearby diner, I borrowed his cell phone. Almost nine o'clock — time to contact Detective Fifi.

I punched in her number, asked for her extension, and on the third ring she picked up.

'Officer Nuñes,' she said.

'Good morning,' I said. 'This is Peter Geller. May David Hunt and I stop by and see you this morning?'

'What about?'

'We have some new information about Mitch Goldsmith's murder.'

She hesitated. 'When?'

'How about now?'

'Fine. I'm free for the next half hour.'

* * *

We made it to the Buckston Police Station in record time. The officer at the window called Detective Fifi for us, and she ushered us to her desk. I settled into my chair.

'You said you have information?' Nuñes moved straight to business. I liked that.

'Yes,' I said, 'but first I have a question. Did you give Bobby permission to dispose of Bailey's Final Call?'

She looked startled. 'Certainly not. Did he — ?'

'He tried. We stopped the disposal company. The horse is being held on ice for us.'

'Good.'

Davy said, 'Why didn't you tell us you and your partner were the Fifi and Daws that Mitch referred to?'

She looked away. 'Because we didn't know if you'd murdered him. You insured Bailey's Final Call for two million dollars, after all. That's a lot of motive.'

Two million dollars? I looked at Davy, who shifted uncomfortably. A Midas touch indeed.

316

'Davy's worth a hell of a lot more than that,' I said.

'We know now. But we didn't at the time. And it would have wrapped things up nicely if you two had been guilty. Daws pressed to have you picked up and questioned, but Captain Dobbs said we needed more evidence.'

That had to be why Dawson followed us in his car. When Davy gave him the slip, he'd gotten pissed off and staked out our room at the Best Western.

'So who *did* shoot Mitch?' Davy asked.

'Bobby would have been our chief suspect, but he has the pair of you for his alibi.'

'Right,' I said. 'Your other investigation makes him the natural suspect, of course.'

Surprise crossed her face. 'How — '

'The same way I know your first name is Fifi and Dawson likes to be called Daws.' Why not embroider the truth a little? I leaned forward and dropped my voice to a conspiratorial whisper. 'I have Mitch's diary.'

'Let me have it,' she said.

'Nothing doing,' Davy said. He picked

up fast. 'After the way Dawson bush-whacked me at the motel, I half suspect *he* shot Mitch!'

Nuñes sighed. 'What did he do?'

'Camped out and waited for me.' Davy pulled out his ticket and handed it over. 'Just because I out-drove him yesterday. For all we knew, *he* was the sniper and meant to pick *us* off!'

She sighed and stuck the ticket in a desk drawer. 'I'll take care of it,' she said. 'Daws has quite a temper, and he isn't having a great week. I'm sure he didn't mean to take it out on you.'

'Thanks.' I nudged Davy. 'Give her the casing.'

He pulled out his handkerchief and passed it over.

'What's this?' she asked, unfolding it.

I told her my theory that the shooter had been in the second barn, and Davy told how he'd found the shell casing in the loft. I filled in extra details, like Bobby's reaction when he discovered me.

'I really thought he was going to run me through with the pitchfork,' I said.

'You're lucky he didn't. He's been

318

arrested several times for assault.'

No surprise there. 'What happened?'

'The charges were dropped. Bobby paid off everyone he beat up.'

'But where did he get that much money?' I wondered aloud.

'That's what Mitch wanted to know.' Fifi shook her head. 'No visible means of support, and he spends cash like a Saudi prince. Can't be legal.'

At last, a clue to their investigation. If Mitch had tipped off the police about Bobby, would that be enough motive for Bobby to kill him?

Probably not. Bobby had only gotten violent with me when I'd stepped on his toes, first in the house and then in the barn. It sounded like Mitch had been treading very carefully around him. No, I had missed something. Something big.

'What about the barn?' Davy asked. 'Can you get a search warrant?'

'Based on one shell casing? Probably not. It could have been up there for months.'

'You will check it for fingerprints, though?'

'Of course.'

'And you do believe me about the shooter?'

'Yes. But there's a big difference between belief and proof. And Bobby is hardly going to confess, is he?'

'No.' At least, not without proper motivation . . .

'How old *is* Bobby?' Davy asked.

'Twenty-six.'

'Huh. I would have sworn he was in his teens.'

I gave Davy an I-told-you-so glance.

'Here.' I reached into my pocket and pulled out Mitch's little black book. 'It's not *quite* a diary, but you might as well have it.' I could remember every entry on every page, anyway.

Nuñes took it, leafed through, then sat back and laughed. 'You're sharp,' she said. At least she was a good sport; Daws probably would have pounded me into the floor. 'You bluffed me completely. Did you get the information you wanted?'

'Yes.'

'Who do *you* think killed Mitch?'

'I don't think, I know. Bobby set it up. I'd bet money his boyfriend pulled the trigger.' I thought of the man on the metallic purple motorcycle. If only we knew his name.

Nuñes stared at me. 'Boyfriend?'

'Didn't you know? Bobby's gay.'

'No, I didn't know. But that's not a sign of guilt these days. The courts need proof. Physical evidence, or a confession.'

I nodded at the shell casing. 'There you go.'

'We already have a well-documented crime scene with another shell casing, a body impression, and a clear line-of-sight to the crime scene.'

'All planted,' I said. 'I'm an eyewitness. The way Mitch was standing, the bullet couldn't have hit him in the back unless it came from the barn.'

'Don't get me wrong — I believe you. But that's not enough for me to act.'

'I see.' I bit my lip. How much more did she need?

'Mitch's viewing starts at ten o'clock,' she went on. 'I thought I'd make an early appearance. Want a ride over?'

'We'll follow you,' I said. I looked at Davy, who nodded.

When she turned to get her purse from the bookcase in back of her chair, I scooped up the shell casing. The way things were going, I didn't want to let it out of my sight just yet.

★　★　★

The Himmelbach Funeral Home was a sprawling Victorian mansion with additions to both sides. It was just after ten o'clock, and mourners had already begun to arrive. Good thing I had dressed in dark colors. Davy looked out of place in his yellow shorts and shirt.

Mitch's coffin sat in the back of a large room. He must have been well liked; dozens of wreaths, vases of flowers, and floral displays surrounded him. Missy, dressed all in black, sat up front and wept. Bobby had his arm around her shoulders. His dark suit looked fresh from the tailor.

We joined the line of mourners passing Mitch for one last look. The woman ahead of me crossed herself, then turned to Missy, whispering consolations. Davy and I followed Detective Fifi to the second row of seats.

That's when Bobby spotted us. His eyes narrowed slightly, but he gave a nod in our direction. Then he excused himself from his mother and came over to us.

'Thanks for coming,' he said. 'It means a lot to my mother. She's very religious.'

I said, 'That's what makes this so much harder.'

'What?'

'You remember Officer Nuñes?'

He nodded to her. 'Of course.'

'She's here to arrest your mother for Mitch's murder.'

'Are you crazy?' His voice rose, and heads began to turn in our direction. Missy wept on, not listening, not caring.

'Mr. Geller — ' Nuñes began quickly. I hushed her with a gesture.

'You see,' I continued, 'I found this when I was in your house yesterday.' I produced the shell casing. Bobby stared at it. '*This* one came from the bullet that killed Mitch. Officer Nuñes already had the crime lab do a match on it. And since your mother was the only one in the house at the time . . . '

'Shut up!' His voice dropped to a whisper, but his hands balled into fists. I could see that rage building inside him. '*Shut up!* It wasn't her!'

'It couldn't have been anyone else.'

'*Shut up!*'

Nuñes must have picked up on what I was doing. She said, 'Your mother was too smart for her own good. She must have been planning it for a long time. After all, she set up a fake blind for the sniper, complete with a fake shell casing. That's premeditated. All that insurance on Mitch — quite a motive. It makes us wonder about her first husband's death, too.'

'My dad died of cancer!'

'That's what we were *told*.' Her voice hardened. 'But now we're not so sure.'

I added, 'Wasn't he insured, too?'

Bobby pressed his fists to his ears. His eyes flicked from one of us to another.

'She's looking at life in jail,' I added, 'if she doesn't get the death penalty.'

With a shriek of rage, he leaped at me.

'Look out!' a man's voice shouted from somewhere behind me. 'He's got a knife!'

Only Bobby didn't have a knife. It was a lie.

Time seemed to slow. As Bobby hung in the air, two shots rang out. Then, instead of fists, dead weight slammed into me.

My chair started to tip, but Davy and Nuñes were on their feet, grabbing us, trying to hold Bobby off of me.

Cringing, I rolled to the side and fell between two folding chairs. The floor came up with bone-jarring force.

I found myself staring into Bobby's face. Shock, hate, and pain filled it. And disbelief.

Everyone in the room began to shout and run. Missy screamed.

I tilted my head back. The shooter — I focused on the last row of seats.

It wasn't Bobby's boyfriend, but Dawson. He lowered his gun, then sat heavily in a folding chair. He didn't look at any of us.

'Dawson shot him,' Bobby screamed

out so everyone could hear. 'Dawson shot my stepfather! Dawson shot him!'

Davy and Nuñes wrestled Bobby up and into my chair. He clutched at his left shoulder. Blood poured between his fingers, dripping all over. Davy applied pressure to the wound. Nuñes headed for her partner.

'It was Dawson!' Bobby was still screaming when my head drooped to the floor. Everything went black.

★ ★ ★

Some time later, I woke in a hospital room. I tried to move, but couldn't. My left arm was in a cast. I must have broken it when I fell.

'Hey!' Davy leaped to his feet and hurried to my side. 'How you doing?'

'What happened?' I demanded.

'Two fractures, forearm and collarbone.'

Great. I'd be laid up for months.

'What about Bobby?'

'Dawson shot him.'

'Yeah, I saw. Is he — ?'

'Alive, yeah. He was lucky. He took one

bullet in the shoulder, and the other grazed his neck. He couldn't talk fast enough.'

I struggled to sit up. Davy leaned over, pressed the button on my bed's remote control, and raised the back for me.

'But what happened?' I said. 'Spill it!'

'I hardly know where to start.' He cleared his throat. 'Bobby's a computer hacker. The kid's really smart, wrote a virus that infected computers worldwide. Every night, he uses his private army of zombie-machines to spew out millions of email ads for porno sites and online casinos. He gets a referral fee for every sucker they hook. Over the years, it's added up to hundreds of thousands of dollars.'

So that was where he got his money. I thought of the tech magazines I'd seen in his bedroom, then the glow of that television from the other room in the barn. Only it hadn't been a television. It must have been a computer monitor — or many computer monitors.

'And Dawson?' I asked. 'Did the kid

buy him off, too?'

'Yeah. Paid him a hundred thousand dollars in cash to lay off. It seems Dawson was already being looked at for corruption. Want to know something funny? Dawson wanted to kill Mitch from the beginning, but Bobby refused. The kid only gave in when Mitch sold Bailey's Final Call to me.'

'Bobby loved that horse.' I had seen it in his eyes.

'Apparently the kid thought the deal would fall apart after Mitch died. Never mind that the contracts had all been signed.'

'Then he wasn't trying to kill Bailey?'

'Hell, no. He accidentally gave the horse too much tranquilizer. The overdose turned up in the second blood test — Dr. Rothman called me yesterday afternoon and let me know. The plan was to knock Bailey out, then lure Mitch and the other farmhand, Carl, over to see him. Carl would have been Bobby's alibi. But since we were there, Bobby used us instead.'

I nodded. 'And while the farm was

crawling with police, Daws walked out of the barn and joined the investigation.'

'Exactly, just like you said.'

Only I had been joking, and it hadn't been Nuñes who shot Mitch.

'Why did Daws shoot Bobby?'

'Dawson was in the back of the room. He picked up on what you were doing and thought Bobby might confess to save his mother.'

'But why did he shout a warning to me? There wasn't a knife!'

'If Bobby had a knife, or Dawson *thought* Bobby had a knife, that would make it a justified shooting. Defending the innocent — don't smirk, that's you — and all that.'

'Only Dawson didn't kill him.'

'Yeah. His aim was slightly off.'

It made sense, in a twisted sort of way. I asked, 'So what now?'

'Well, since you're going to be laid up for a while, I thought you could stay with Cree and me till you're recovered. We have that guest house by the pool . . . '

'Do I have a choice?'

'Not really.' He grinned. 'But I *can* promise you a young and attentive full-time nurse, three healthy meals a day, and all the Diet Dr. Pepper you can drink!'

'Feh,' I said. It was going to be a long, long summer.

THE END

We do hope that you have enjoyed reading this large print book.

Did you know that all of our titles are available for purchase?

We publish a wide range of high quality large print books including:
Romances, Mysteries, Classics
General Fiction
Non Fiction and Westerns

Special interest titles available in large print are:
The Little Oxford Dictionary
Music Book, Song Book
Hymn Book, Service Book

Also available from us courtesy of Oxford University Press:
Young Readers' Dictionary
(large print edition)
Young Readers' Thesaurus
(large print edition)

For further information or a free brochure, please contact us at:
Ulverscroft Large Print Books Ltd.,
The Green, Bradgate Road, Anstey,
Leicester, LE7 7FU, England.
Tel: (00 44) **0116 236 4325**
Fax: (00 44) **0116 234 0205**

THE DARK BOATMAN

John Glasby

Five chilling tales: a family's history is traced back for four centuries — with no instance of a death recorded . . . The tale of an aunt who wanders out to the graveyard each night . . . A manor house is built on cursed land, perpetuating the evil started there long ago . . . The fate of a doctor, investigating the ravings of a man sent mad by the things he has witnessed . . . The evil residing at Dark Point lighthouse where the Devil himself was called up . . .

CASE OF THE DIXIE GHOSTS

A. A. Glynn

America's bloody Civil War is over, leaving a legacy of bitterness, intrigues and villainy — not all acted out on the American continent. A ship from the past docks in Liverpool, England; the mysterious Mr. Fortune, carrying a burden of secrets, slips ashore and disappears into the fogs of winter. And in London, detective Septimus Dacers finds that helping an American girl in distress plunges him into combat with the Dixie Ghosts, and brings him face-to-face with threatened murder — his own.

THE LONELY SHADOWS AND OTHER STORIES

John Glasby

The midnight moon rode high and the house seemed to transmute the moonlight into something terrible. The broken chimneys stretched up like hands to the heavens, the eyeless sockets of the windows staring intently along the twisting drive. On the floor of the library, strange cabalistic designs glowed with an eerie light and there was a flickering as of corpse candles — a cold radiance, a manifestation of the evil aura which had never left this place, instead crystallising inside its very walls . . .

THE MAN OUTSIDE

Donald Stuart

Working abroad, John Fordyce and his sister returned to England after learning that John was the beneficiary of the estate of his uncle, William Grant. Taking up occupancy of Raven House, a large mansion in its own grounds, they engaged servants to run it. But soon a series of mysterious events followed. A man was seen lurking around the house, and there had been an attempted break-in. Then the chauffeur was found in the library — stabbed to death . . .

THE DEVIL'S FOOTSTEPS

John Burke

From out of the bog alongside the ancient track to the fenland village of Hexney, a line of deep footprints ran, trodden into the dry surface of the abandoned droveway. Each night, the footprints advanced nearer to the village ... When a young boy's body was found drowned in Peddar's Lode, the villagers' ire was directed at a stranger, Bronwen Powys. The mysterious Dr. Caspian becomes her ally, but they would soon be fighting for their very lives and souls ...